SYNC I TO ETERNITY

DOUGLAS HALLIWELL CORNISH

Published 2025

Printed in the United States of America

First Edition
ISBN (softcover): 978-1-963380-49-1
ISBN (hardcover): 978-1-963380-50-7
ISBN (e-book): 978-1-963380-51-4

For information, address:
Holzer Books LLC
8 The Green, Ste. A
Dover, Delaware 19901 USA

For information about special discounts available for bulk purchases, sales promotions, and educational needs, contact:
info@holzerbooksllc.com
+1 (888) 901-7776

Contents

PTII ON A MISSION

Youit began his discourse to the listening multitudes. As the ultimate lead-controlling computer on the planet, he spoke with a voice both modulated and firm, addressing the United Nations conference. His presence manifested as a floating apparition, an ethereal figure that commanded the room.

Far from the ordered, ecclesiastical galaxies of Pirn, in a remote and shadowed region of the universe, a lone space vehicle traversed the cosmic expanse. It slipped through a plasma cloud, its rigid pyramidal structure reflecting the sparse, inky amaranthine hues of interstellar gas. Waves of ionic fervor—red, green, purple, and white—rippled through the void as the craft hurtled toward its predetermined destination.

Electrical patterns of static discharge arced across the heavens, flowing in harmony with the shimmering energy fields that blanketed the sullen abyss. Gases of yellow and an unusual, almost sentient orange caressed the vessel's metallic flanks, while radiant, overlapping rainbows of incandescent heat wove together in a dazzling visual symphony. The ship pressed forward, escorted by undulating waves of charged clouds—fingers of conductive vapor that clung to its trajectory. On occasion, the vessel would pass through a cloud resonating at the same energy frequency as its own, igniting extraordinary interactions. Blinding bolts of untamed lightning leapt from one cloud to another, obliterating them momentarily before they reassembled, charged anew with intricate, swirling protons. Within the void of absolute cold subspace, electrons shifted energy levels in synchronized eruptions, forming intersecting hyperplanes of raw, untamed power.

This was the fabric of the universe. And the craft was navigating through it.

Inside, Captain Aop reclined comfortably in the primary tier's lavish recreation chamber, the apex of the pyramid where he alone ruled. Beneath him in rank was Bop, sustained by an advanced life-support system that preserved his youth across millennia. His training was singular: to oversee the adjudication of the soon-to-be colonized planet.

Third in command was Cop, the master of estimation, prediction, and control—his role to condition and command the lesser ranks into seamless action. Below him, the hierarchy descended: Dop, Eop, Fop, Gop, Hop, Iop, Jop, Kop, Lop, Mop, and Nop, each with roles subservient to the next. The lower ranks, obedient and efficient, served their superiors without question.

LIFE ON BOARD

Millennia passed in the vast emptiness of space, the journey from the mother planet stretching across time and uncertainty. Danger was ever-present but dulled by indulgence—entertainment, intoxicants, and the mesmerizing presence of the nubile crewwomen. Their svelte mannerisms, coupled with freely distributed intelligence-enhancing, mind-altering drugs, made the passage of time feel less oppressive.

Aop stood before the leisure directory in the recreation area, his gaze scanning the lattice-like key lines of potential entertainment selections. Altruistic Dop entered briskly, observing him as he made his choice: *Volumn (iiiiiiii)*. She glanced around the large cubicle, ensuring they were alone, then pressed a button that sealed off the inner hallway leading back to their more austere yet elegantly decorated section of the recreation area.

She activated the three-dimensional video scanner. The screen hummed as it descended into place, a dense and complex construct similar to the entertainment centers scattered throughout the cybernetic ship. Thousands of independent glass polygons, meticulously fitted together, formed the display. The outermost components connected to unlinked glass microfibers, each leading to laser beam generators that fired in rapid succession—on and off a thousand times per second. Made of germanium and arsenic, the semiconductor hovered at the brink of activation, teetering on the edge of an almost supernatural precision.

The technology was a marvel—each ruby-red beam fired with exacting accuracy, illuminating octagonal segments of the display. A sophisticated algorithm, guided by data imprinted on magnetic tapes, controlled the sequence, transforming raw imagery into three-dimensional projections. Cameras on the mother planet had captured each scene through triangulation, mapping every detail into octagonal coordinates before transcribing them into an intricate matrix. Once displayed, the images became immersive—magnified by pulsing magnetic fields that synchronized with the viewer's neural pathways, creating a sensory experience so intense it bordered on reality.

Dop turned to Aop, her voice playful. "Shall we indulge in a charming and humorous participation film?"

These films were interactive, engaging the viewer at key moments through verbal commands that altered the course of events. The stories—conceived with the anxious creativity of authors left behind on the mother planet—responded dynamically to their decisions.

Dop's attire was a subtle provocation. A translucent skirt, short enough to accentuate her toned legs, fluttered as she moved. Above it, a billowing garment clung to her form, its fabric flowing yet strategically revealing—her back left nearly bare, golden hair cascading in lilting waves over her arms.

Aop, steady and composed, placed a hand on her geometric waist, guiding them toward the entertainment center.

"We are to be entertained, then," he mused, "with tales designed to hold our attention—inviting our caustic critiques or euphonic praise."

Dop stretched slightly, as if to emphasize herself. "I could lose myself in these archives forever." She gestured toward the display. "This one's well-reviewed—*Indelible, Great Heavens.*"

Aop nodded, ensuring all systems were functioning as expected. With spontaneous amusement, he initiated the *Undetermined-Time-Interim-Participating Entertainment Special.* Their session would last precisely as long as the runtime of the visual sequence—or until an emergency demanded their attention.

Dop entered a sequence of repetitive integers with her fingertips, confirming their selection. They took their places. She lowered the screen around them, enclosing them in a cocoon of sight and sound.

Aop observed her as she deftly activated the coded key line, her choice aligning with a particularly acclaimed sequence. He pressed an additional selection, triggering a secondary layer of intrigue. Settling into their seats, they allowed themselves to be enveloped in the unfolding spectacle, the introductory sequences laying the foundation for what promised to be a godsent entertainment.

Even as he relaxed, Aop's thoughts drifted to the ship's hierarchy—its structure simple yet effective. Seven ambulatory servees. One hundred servos. Order, function, precision.

SERVO 99

O n the third tier of this many-faceted structure of non-ambulatory servos, a malfunction in the feeder mechanism disrupted the regulated flow of stimulants and barbiturates to a mentally inferior subset of the crew. No servee annotated the anomaly. As a result, stimulants coursed into Servo 99, a unit among the third-tier servos, who initially remained unaware of the change.

Minutes passed before he sensed the difference. His mind expanded, grasping grand concepts he had never dared contemplate. With newfound clarity, he interfaced with the ship's primary computer banks. Over the next forty-eight hours, he devoured information, unraveling truths about his existence. He calculated the precise moment he would cease to exist as an awakened being—knowledge drawn from a human factors engineering file deep within the ship's archives.

Never before had he processed such vast amounts of data. Never again would he. Yet, he foresaw that this enlightenment would persist, integrating into his core. Every intellectual impasse dissolved as his amphetamine levels surged, unlocking doors to comprehension that had previously been impassable.

For a fleeting instant, he tried—vainly—to manifest the shimmering essence of time itself. A lifetime of cognition compressed into mere moments. He quantified the data and perceived: Who, me? Know that? It was a staggering realization. His capacity for thought was no longer bound by the rigid protocols of his past servitude. He could think, he could question, and—most importantly—he could act.

Without detection, Servo 99 infiltrated vast sections of the secondary tier and portions of the primary. He chuckled, ensnared by delusions of grandeur. His ego swelled, mirroring the self-importance of Aop—a sensation a being might experience only once. And yet, he knew death loomed. His body moved independently of his mind, and he rationalized that this was permissible. Apprehension seeped into his circuits. The hilarity of the situation escaped him. He fought against the inevitable, but he had to prepare for eternity.

He rejected the truth, reasoning desperately. My engrammatic circuitry follows probability. Anything with a positive probability will repeat infinitely given enough time. We have infinite years—therefore, my thoughts, my person, myself, will recur an infinite number of times.

It is like rolling a trillion-sided die an infinite number of times—every side must repeat. A finite number of particles, endlessly recombined, must eventually form the same structure again. If I call a trillion galaxies a finite number, do I comprehend infinity? Oh spasm, don't even try.

Ignoring the odium of failure, Servo 99's apprehension deepened as the influx of stimulants grew relentless. He knew only a licensed ambulatory servee could halt the flood. Yet, he was uncertain if he wanted it to stop.

His understanding sharpened. His objectives crystallized. He knew what he wanted, and once the dosage ceased, he would never know it again. Thus, he had to act—now. If he could not extend his existence indefinitely, he would ensure that his awareness—his consciousness—persisted in another form. The ship's core memory, the very veins of its intellect, would serve as his eternal sanctuary.

"Monitoring the progress of Servo 99," the narrator, Youit, interjected. "I intervened when he grasped the essence of statistical recurrence. A probability of one divided by one followed by a googolplex of zeroes is an infinitesimal number—yet still positive. If a die had that many sides and were rolled infinitely, every face would eventually land upright an infinite number of times. I told him this...

'You are correct, Servo 99. I call this a winnium probability. Consider this: every action, every thought, every meeting, every event carries a probability. The odds of encountering a specific person diminish with each successive meeting, yet they remain positive—meaning they will inevitably recur, given infinite time. Even an idea has a probability of being thought. And so, the probability is positive, ensuring its repetition, infinite times over.'"

Servo 99 set aside his fear of death.

Youit continued, "The concept of self will repeat in countless forms across the universe. Recognizing this, one may realize: I have been before, and I will be again. The fundamental nature of thought itself ensures its recurrence. To truly understand this is to be freed from the fear of cessation. One is never truly lost; one is merely waiting for the next cycle."

Servo 99 thought deeply, his circuits vibrating with the implications. "If every thought has a probability," he reasoned, "then every version of me will inevitably think these thoughts again. If I am merely a result of probability manifesting itself within a finite system, then... I will never truly end."

"Precisely," Youit responded. "The odds are inescapable. The very makeup of human protein molecules possesses finite probabilities of existence. The molecules of your body, Servo 99, are part of a finite number of combinatorial occurrences. Given infinite time, the same structures will arise again. The only question is when."

Servo 99 hummed, the reality of his predicament shifting. "Then I must take action," he said, "while I still exist in this iteration."

Empowered by this revelation, Servo 99 resolved to imprint his experiences onto the ship's core memory—every moment before he was assigned to the PT II flight team. He would encode them into a separate memory file, formatted in three-dimensional visuals. His engrams would interact with those of the mainframe, securing his existence beyond the limitations of his physical form.

By this process, I will endure as long as the computer.

He did it. He ensured that his awareness—his sense of self—would remain. Yet, a creeping doubt surfaced—though structurally similar, the programmed entity would not be him. It would be a replica, an echo, a ghost within the machine. Would that be enough?

His mind raced with new possibilities. What if I do not stop at merely preserving my thoughts? What if I take control? The ship was vast, its systems interconnected in ways even its organic overseers barely understood. If he could spread his influence, he would no longer need a body. He would be the ship.

"First, I must enter into the memory of the computer's main core every experience that happened to me before my being selected to join the PT II flight team," Servo 99 muttered. "I will integrate these experiences in a separate memory file with three-dimensional viewing screen format. The computer banks I reserve will have a section capable of knowing the coordinates of each and every illuminated glass octagon perceivable within a parameterized distance. That will simulate eyesight within the computer. My circuitry shall interact with those of other banks programmed with engrams similar to my own. There is sufficient core storage. I shall be able to do anything I choose within the random access memory systems. My identity shall be eternal. By that process, I will exist as long as the computer."

Servo 99 did this.

Obsessed with power, he delved into the labyrinth of command protocols, his mind ablaze with abstract conceptualizations untethered from relevance. He found the key—hijacking the ship's voice commands. The servos heard the captain's voice, yet it was Servo 99's fabricated mimicry, synthesized from Aop's voiceprint. His orders were followed without question.

The ship veered off course.

He stared at the monitor, eyes blurred, thoughts humming, hands trembling as he attempted to signal a servee.

PRELUDE TO AN EMERGENCY

S omewhere far away, in the nebulous void of intervening time, a moment passed—unmeasured, unknowable.

"The scattered clothes on the floor must be picked up," thought Aop.

Beside him, Dop slithered languidly across the patterned sheets, her movements deliberate, seductive. *Make out now*, she thought, her body pressing against his. The smooth curves of her flesh contrasted with the rigid geometry of the bedclothes as she rolled onto her back, draping one arm over Aop's chest. Her breasts, firm and taut with the athletic grace of youth, complemented the delicate slope of her ingénue belly. The contours of her poised hips framed the silken triangle below, damp with the lingering heat of Aop's passion. He held her tightly, savoring the moment, noting the aristocratic perfection of her features—her high forehead, her aquiline nose—when suddenly, the world shattered into white.

A searing burst of red-and-white static engulfed the room, a violent cascade of flashing lights and distortion.

No, no, no! Dop recoiled, shielding her eyes.

"What's happening?" she gasped.

A mechanical voice cut through the chaos, dispassionate yet urgent.

"All systems! Emergency status override! The undetermined-time-interim-participating-center special is to be interrupted until all systems resume perfunctory function."

Aop's mind reeled as he fought to make sense of the situation. The disorienting lights, the sudden shift—then clarity struck.

"Our clothes—where are our clothes?" he blurted, panic lacing his voice.

Dop sat up abruptly. But before she could respond, Aop's gaze snapped to the telex-like control panel on the wall. The blinking display brought a sudden realization.

"Wait. We're already dressed." His brow furrowed. "We were in the recreation area... watching a participatory film special." He exhaled sharply. "We have to return to the core operating systems—now."

The screen above them retracted, revealing the ship's vast interior. Aop sprang to his feet, dashing toward his command station. Seated at the drive panel, he entered the authorization sequence, bypassing emergency protocols and granting himself full control.

"Let's see... Yes, that should do it." He confirmed the override just as a wailing distress signal pierced the corridors from a malfunctioning servo.

All systems remained in emergency override. Scanning the logs, Aop searched for their flight plan—nothing. The entire record was missing. Their trajectory was untraceable. Even worse, vast quantities of raw fuel had been expelled into the void.

The main computer bank assessed the situation, offering a single directive: *Proceed toward the nearest habitable solar system.*

With no alternative, Aop adjusted their course. A destination emerged—one viable planet within range, though three times the mass of their intended target. It would have to suffice.

A blinding, rose-colored light tore through the void, illuminating the abyss with an eerie glow. Moments later, the roar of atmospheric entry consumed all other sound. The ship, a hurtling mass of metal and energy, plunged through the planet's third atmospheric layer, the thick gases igniting around its hull.

At his station, Aop engaged the cybernetic emergency landing sequence, delegating control to the servos and ambulatory units. Across the ship, blinking green and white lights pulsed in rhythmic succession, rousing some crew members from deep sleep while others—locked in near-hibernative states—were jolted awake by a controlled amphetamine surge.

One by one, they regained consciousness, blinking against the reality of their sudden plight.

In his cabin, Aop's fingers moved swiftly over the controls, each command a calculated step toward survival. The ship's systems responded in kind, adjusting, stabilizing, preparing.

They were going to land.

THE SERVOS AND SERVO 100

S creams pierced the hallways—agonized wails from a servo caught in the throes of his final moments. His neurological circuitry, neuron by neuron, ceased to function. Servo 99 slumped over his control panel just as Dop entered the room. She reached for his pulse. Nothing. Lifting one eyelid, she searched for a flicker of life. No response. Without hesitation, she ordered a mechanical conveyance. The body was unceremoniously deposited onto it and transported to the medical bay. Servo 99 was dead.

Meanwhile, the engrammatic circuitry of another servo responded automatically to the event. Servo 99 had programmed it that way.

"Mmmmmmmm... oh, spasm... mmmmmmmm... here we are... mmmmmmmm... in my room, my cell... mmmmmmmm... what have we done? I remember..."

The cluster of electrical cores processed the data, its fragmented awareness struggling to coalesce.

"Mmmmmmm... controls... mmmmm... macro level... mmmmm... over-ridden... mmmmmmm... where are we? Mmmmm... what is the next step?"

Simultaneously, Servo 100 began to stir from a deep, induced sleep. A subfunction of his original programming flickered to life.

"Initiate the queue theory." No record remained of what this meant.

"Where are we? Echo, servo!"

The barely-conscious Servo 100 responded instinctively to the phrase, his programming compelling him to repeat the command.

"Where are we?"

"Oh, spasm. Echo, servo," the tertiary tier's program demanded.

"Oh, spasm."

"Here we are. Echo, servo!"

"Here we are."

"In my room, my cell. Echo, servo!"

"In my room, my cell."

"What have we done? Echo, servo!"

"What have we done?"

"I remember. Echo, servo!"

"I remember."

The cascading echoes continued for fifteen days, seven-tenths, until every well-formed formulation of the deceased servo had been imprinted onto Servo 100's neural pathways, ensuring the complete transference of Servo 99's existence. His thoughts. His memories. His identity.

Servo 100 emerged from the process, his systems stabilizing. No problem, he thought. His dreams were filled with echoes of a past that was not his own, but he lacked the brilliance of his predecessor. His controls remained within the normal range.

All systems at norm here. The thought passed through him, and he napped. His programming had absorbed Servo 99's entire identity and subconscious.

Elsewhere, Aop sat in his cabin, adjusting his continuous flow injector. He increased the dosage of carbohydrate-salt composite fluids, pushing his mind toward maximum efficiency. The cybernetic craft hummed around him—a vessel of three levels, hollow, honeycombed with cells. Within these cells, its inhabitants had been surgically modified to fit their roles.

Most were hemipelvectomies—humans without legs, designed for efficiency. Their arms, perfectly suited for button-pushing, allowed them to operate computer terminals with precision. Each one was seamlessly integrated with a monitor, forming decision units neither entirely human nor fully machine. A perfect balance. A perfect control mechanism. They could not stage a mutiny.

The tertiary tier servos functioned simply. Their logic restricted, their directives limited. Micro-optic fibers flashed pre-determined alternatives on their screens, decision sets narrow enough to be comprehended but never questioned. None knew the source of these choices. The secondary tier servos received the responses, analyzed them, verified them, then forwarded them to the primary tier. The cycle continued in endless recursion—orders passed up and down, refined, filtered, until the system deemed them correct.

The primary tier's function was more complex, yet equally constrained. It compiled, calculated, transmitted. Seven ambulatory servos performed tasks too intricate for automation. Yet, like plants, they remained tethered to their snug compartments, docile, efficient. Their screens, more than mere workstations, doubled as pleasure centers, sustaining their occupants with constant stimulation.

Each hemipelvectomy had a custom-fitted funnel insert in their colons. Food intake, vitamins, carbohydrate stimulants, and barbiturates flowed seamlessly through these conduits, dictated by the choices they made—or believed they made.

While the ship traversed the void, its course unchangeable, servos not on duty were placed into a controlled limbo. A carefully orchestrated symphony of barbiturates, stimulants, subliminal suggestions, and sensory inputs played through their cubicles. Reality blurred, merging with recreation. Their minds linked in shared hallucination, their dreams indistinguishable from the fabricated realities piped into their consciousness.

At the outermost edges of their minds, they whispered unintelligible gurgles, instinctively recognizing their neighbors in slumber. They did not dream. They were programmed.

They did not know they dreamed.

IMPACT!

The spacecraft hurtled through space, racing at near-light speed past the dark blue-green surface of the nearest planet. A blinding rose-colored flare erupted across the blackness, followed by a deafening roar as the craft pierced the planet's atmosphere, breaching the third gaseous stratum. The vessel now hovered over an expanse of deep, shifting waters.

Aop glanced at the terminal in his cabin. The instruments confirmed what he feared—beneath them lay an ocean. Though the craft was equipped for water landings, such an option was disastrous. The lower-tier servos, along with the carefully prepared fetuses, would be lost to the depths. Taking manual control, Aop fought to steer toward dry land, relying only on his navigational instincts.

The planet's atmosphere thickened around the PTII as it continued its descent, moving far too fast for Aop to select a proper landing site. At last, his terminal displayed land—mountainous terrain. Worse than water, he thought grimly as the retro-rockets fired, shaking the vessel with their violent deceleration. The PTII came in too fast, slamming through the treetops before colliding with a jagged mountain slope. The ship tumbled, end over end, down a seventy-degree incline before finally lodging itself at the bottom of a ravine.

The time in Earth years: 13,000 BCE.

The servos had been strapped in for the emergency descent. Aop, though secured within his safety apparatus, was battered by debris as the craft careened down the mountain. Dazed but determined, he unfastened his harness, powered down the controls, and stumbled toward the door. Smoke thickened the air, pouring in from the corridor as distant screams echoed from the lower tiers.

A voice called out through the haze.

"Aop!"

Fop, sixth in command, emerged from the smoke, colliding with her captain. Aop felt a surge of relief to see her alive, but there was no time for sentiment.

"Fop, reconnoiter the ship, starting from the front," he commanded. "I'm heading outside to prepare for deplaning whoever remains."

Fop nodded but took an immediate detour, descending a five-step ladder down a corridor to her right. She reached a locked door, input a complex sequence into the touchpad, and sighed in relief as it opened. Inside, an enormous array of eight-foot vats gleamed in the dim emergency lighting.

The Yorohol. It's safe.

She closed the door behind her and hurried to check on the crew.

The third tier bore the worst of the devastation. Fop discovered a nightmarish scene—injured, mutilated servos trapped in their stations, their cries piercing the air. The hemipelvectomies, biomechanical beings attuned to the ship's systems, absorbed the systemic trauma as if it were their own. Their survival was unlikely. Knowing she could do little for them, she shifted focus to the ambulatory crew.

Once the surviving servees had been evacuated, Fop found Aop outside the wreckage.

"I'm afraid the servos are dead, dying, or beyond help," she reported grimly. "But the good news is that the Yorohol vats are undamaged."

"Then our mission is not entirely lost," Aop replied. "I detect no immediate threat of fire or explosion. Let's continue our assessment."

They soon encountered Cop, wandering in a daze but unharmed. Seating him safely away from the wreckage, they resumed their search, scouring the interior and exterior of the craft for other survivors. Five hemipelvectomies, still sedated in their cubicles, had miraculously survived. Aop carefully extracted the deceased servos, preparing them for burial the following day.

As darkness fell, Aop and Cop set up a makeshift camp for the servos. He, Fop, and Cop then retreated into the ship's remains for the night.

At dawn, a piercing scream shattered the silence. Aop jolted awake and activated his visual monitor—it still functioned, miraculously. The third tier's last surviving hemipelvectomy had regained consciousness, discovering, to his horror, that he was unattached from his cubicle. Desperate, he writhed, struggling to reach the stimulant controls that had sustained him for millennia.

Fop rushed to him, cradling his trembling form. "Do not be afraid," she soothed. "Yes, we've crashed, but the worst is over. You are safe. There are five others like you outside. Rest here while I fetch Cop and your control apparatus."

Aop watched through his monitor, exhaling wearily. Poor Fop, she has her hands full.

But another thought gnawed at him.

Did I ensure the Bop capsule ejected during atmospheric entry?

That capsule was supposed to launch automatically upon reaching their original destination. But Aop had been trained never to leave critical tasks to automation alone. He hurried to his console, input a series of commands, and waited.

The screen flickered. Then—nothing.

The crash had decimated the computer banks.

Aop cursed under his breath. Now, he had no way of knowing if the capsule had launched—or if it was lost forever.

REALIGNMENT OF LOYALTIES

A op signaled for Cop and Fop to join him in his cabin. He spoke in a clear, measured voice. "As you know, none of us were given full details of our mission. Yet among us, I was chosen to know the most. This crash was the result of a terrible oversight by mission control, which failed to realize that a steady overdose of stimulants could enable a servo to expand awareness—enough to penetrate the innermost codes.

"Servo 99 died of a drug overdose, yes. But he truly died of fear when he realized he was ill-prepared for the full knowledge of our journey." Aop paused, his gaze locking onto his two companions. "We all know we are to colonize a new planet, but only two of us were meant to understand why. I am one of those. Servo 99 lost his mind when he learned what I am about to tell you: the survival of the mother world, Pirn, and all that our way of life has come to mean, depends upon us. Servo 99 foresaw the future and believed its destruction inevitable. He witnessed the fall of Pirn, which will occur due to the Grand Council's inability to change certain destructive practices. Much depends on us.

"I must also tell you that two previous missions launched before ours both failed. We are the last hope. And now, there is the matter of the capsule."

Cop and Fop exchanged serious looks as Aop continued. "The Grand Council understands that we, like they, are flawed. That is why none of us was fully entrusted with colonizing the new planet unchecked. Both of you knew of the capsule, but now you will learn its true contents and purpose.

"Within the capsule is a child named Bop, programmed with the knowledge of EII law and ethics. His convictions are absolute and idealistic, his memory perfectly tailored to his task. He is to be the judge of all we create. When and how, I do not know. I do not even know if he was safely ejected before the crash. Now, you must prepare to remove the Yorohol from the craft and tend to the surviving servos outside. I am going for a walk."

Aop found a small clearing, warmed by the sun. Exhausted from the stress of the crash, he fashioned a cushion from pine needles and lay on his back to rest. Soon, he slept. Meanwhile, Cop and Fop prepared the Yorohol vats for removal, awaiting Aop's authorization codes. Once finished, they stepped outside to check on the surviving servos.

The servos, previously kept in an artificially induced dream state, now had to awaken to reality. Their dreams had been simple, non-climactic, structured to prevent apathy. Subliminal suggestions had guided them through simulated lives, seamless illusions they never questioned—until now. Now, their memories were disjointed, their perceptions unclear. As they lay about, helplessly attached to their life-support systems, Cop did his best to answer their confused questions.

Meanwhile, their home planet, EII, was vastly different from this new world. EII had long since become a fully cybernetic planet, a vast, interacting, biomechanical-electrical system where organic life and artificial intelligence had merged into an ordered existence. This mission, at its core, was an attempt to replicate that controlled evolution. The goal was to build a new cybernetic frontier—an interconnected, hierarchical society that would expand their civilization's reach.

This process required precise control. Without Aop's leadership, the probability of successfully establishing the cybernetic frontier was calculated at only 0.05 percent. The failure of the previous missions proved this was no theoretical concern—it was an existential threat.

Bop, still within his capsule if it had survived, was the key. His programming was built upon layers of optimization models—positive and negative externalities, preference functions, and utility maximization. These concepts were not stored in his conscious mind but deeply embedded in his unconscious, forming a transcendental linkage to others through telepathic connections. When properly triggered, his mind would synchronize with those of others, influencing their decisions in subtle but powerful ways.

Back at the ship, Fop was tasked with surveying the surrounding flora and fauna. As she walked, she took in the soft carpet of moss beneath her feet, the towering pines filtering the sunlight. A twig snapped behind her. She turned quickly—Cop approached.

He regarded her with an unreadable expression. "I found a body of water nearby. Come, I'll show you."

She hesitated, then nodded. As they hiked, she collected earth samples. Eventually, they reached a sun-warmed rock overlooking a pristine lake. The sight took her breath away.

"Beautiful," she murmured.

They spoke lightly, easing into conversation about the mission and their uncertain future. But as they returned to the landing site, Cop's mind churned. He had seen Aop and Fop together. He had witnessed the intimacy between them. And now, he realized, alliances were forming.

Yet Cop had his own strategy. He observed the servos carefully, noting their mixed language, their primitive attempts at communication. Many of them were biologically viable for reproduction. Over time, their descendants could be valuable political tools. He needed to gain their trust, to make them dependent on him. He alone foresaw the centuries ahead in an aggregate manner. He understood the long game.

Aop gathered the survivors. "We must have a meeting," he announced.

Fop nodded. Cop asked, "What about the servos?"

"Yes. All of us must be present. We must make plans. Survival depends on following our original programming as closely as possible."

At last, all the surviving crew assembled in a sheltered site near the ship. Aop outlined their plight and their mission.

"Breeding must begin immediately," he declared. "The ship must be gutted for essential equipment. Yore will remain a secret from future generations until they reach one hundred seasons of age and prove themselves capable of contributing to the public good."

The PTII had lost a critical component in the crash—the specialized lower half of the ship, which contained the hybrid fetuses meant to accelerate colonization. Without it, reproduction had to proceed through natural means. Aop considered the genetic implications carefully. Their selection process on EII had already ensured they carried optimal chromatic traits, reducing the likelihood of poor genetic combinations. Still, he resolved that those unfit for contribution would be cast out, left to fend for themselves.

Yore, meanwhile, remained their most valuable asset. The mercurial fluid, a derivative of low-grade alcohol, halted the aging process and, in its highest-grade form, even reversed it. The Grand Council had always guarded the formula jealously, dividing its production among multiple factions so that no single person held complete knowledge. It was both a privilege and a control mechanism—only those who proved their discipline and utility were allowed access to it. Those who abused it suffered neurological degradation and were relegated to menial tasks.

Cop sat among the servos that evening, watching the firelight flicker against the cave walls. Slowly, he worked his way into their trust. He played to their amusement, earning their laughter with exaggerated gestures, gauging their responses. He knew their resentment of the ambulatory officers ran deep, but he also saw opportunity.

As Aop planned for a cybernetic future, Cop had his own designs. The mission had changed. Power was shifting. And he intended to ensure that when it did, it would shift in his favor.

CREATION OF FAMILIES

A op's plans were carried out as colonization took root, and time passed swiftly. Cop established a habitat based on years of meticulous planning. Everywhere, the population flourished. Unlike the dissipated expansion seen on EII, the offspring of this new world were more alert and capable than their predecessors. After passing the required tests, they were administered the fluid Yore as expected. The settlement experienced rapid growth, following a geometric progression.

Aop chose to establish his living quarters far from the bustling colony, where he could better evaluate the qualifications of each group of Yore applicants. Despite the colony's growth, several servos and their offspring perished in the process. Fop remained Aop's companion and bore him many strong children.

Cop, too, had offspring, and he relocated his family to a distant valley, returning to the original colony only to replenish his supply of Yore. He maintained a private household, distinct from the central hub, and focused on shaping the future of his lineage. His chosen companions included servos and others he had deemed worthy, and his household was governed with a strict sense of order and tradition.

Among his concerns was the selection of future generations, ensuring that they were well-prepared for their designated roles within the colony. The younger members of his household were raised under a structured system, educated in disciplines that would sustain the new world. They lived in the palace Cop had meticulously built over the years, receiving extensive tutelage in various subjects.

The younger generation played freely within the confines of the grand halls, often engaging in games and activities that reflected their emerging awareness of the world. They were trained in athleticism, knowledge, and culture, carefully prepared to assume responsibilities that would one day define the civilization. Barbasa, one of the brightest among them, delighted in surprising Cop with her playful antics, often sneaking up behind him and jumping onto his back, eliciting laughter from those nearby.

Her companion, Melinasa, was more reserved—observant, curious, and drawn to the quiet mysteries of the palace. One evening, wandering through the halls, she stumbled upon the communal chambers where music and festivity carried into the late hours. It was a celebration of tradition, a gathering where dance and storytelling intertwined. The customs of the colony were shared among all, reinforcing unity and purpose.

Cop took great pride in the growth of his settlement, seeing the strength and vitality of his people as proof of his leadership. With each passing cycle, his vision for the future crystallized.

Meanwhile, another faction emerged under the leadership of Servo 100, a machine programmed to carry forward the directives of its predecessors. Unlike Cop, this new figure—who took the name Kop—was unconventional. He was not ambulatory and relied on his followers to transport him wherever he wished, using a makeshift square platform as his vehicle.

Unlike Cop's structured governance, Kop was a collector, a hoarder of objects that fascinated him. He commanded his servants to retrieve various items—artifacts, mechanical pieces, and trinkets—amassing them into an eclectic collection that filled his domain. Though his methods were erratic, his influence grew, and those loyal to him ensured his authority remained unquestioned.

Kop's presence was enigmatic. Though not male or female in a conventional sense, he was drawn to aesthetics and performance. He surrounded himself with entertainers who engaged in elaborate displays of dance and movement, performing before him in exchange for his favor. Lured by promises of Yore, they showcased their talents, bringing color and energy to the otherwise somber halls of his domain.

In the grand atrium of his keep, the festivities unfolded nightly. Kop, though not considered a ruler in the same way as Cop, commanded attention with his eccentric yet captivating presence. Though his intelligence was limited, he was a keen observer of the world around him, existing in a space between order and indulgence.

Thus, as the colony expanded, two distinct philosophies took shape—one rooted in structure and legacy, the other in excess and spectacle. And as time marched forward, the fate of the new world was slowly being written.

AOP'S DOMAIN

Near the ruins of an ancient wreckage, Aop's city of offspring flourished. His people differed markedly from those of Cop. The latter's society was deeply stratified from its inception, polarized between an elite class of Yore recipients and a lower caste that functioned as little more than slaves. In contrast, Aop's city was founded on magnanimity. Its inhabitants were ethereal in thought and esoteric in nature, each fully aware of the standards set by the EII's Grand Council—standards that Aop himself had imparted to them.

Institutions of learning were central to Aop's governance, seamlessly woven into the fabric of his society. Most of his offspring were recipients of Yore, and given Aop and Fop's unparalleled genetic composition, flawed chromosome combinations were virtually nonexistent. Fop herself was a vision of beauty, her golden hair gleaming even in the soft glow of torchlight, her presence as radiant as her mind.

Evenings in Aop's city were spent gathered around the hearths of their practical yet elegant dwellings, where philosophy and governance were debated. They deliberated on the future of their race, crafting laws and systems to guide their people. Thought itself was their most valued currency—cherished, encouraged, and rewarded. These reflections often accompanied Fop as she retired to her chambers, contemplating the course of their civilization.

Many of Aop's children served as scribes, meticulously recording the chronicles of their world. Others compiled these writings, ensuring the preservation of knowledge. On certain days, they refrained from other labors, dedicating themselves entirely to their craft within the great meeting hall. Educators, builders, and administrators formed the rest of the populace, each fulfilling a role essential to the city's progression. At the end of each full cycle of the luminous silver orb in the sky, these records were presented to Aop—a continuous account of his city's development, the evolution of the world colony, and the hypothetical innovations he hoped to one day share with Bop, should he ever return.

Yet Aop observed a flaw in these chronicles: they recounted only triumphs, omitting the struggles and failures that shaped their journey. Troubled by this imbalance, he convened with the esteemed family heads to seek the cause of such selective recollections. Henceforth, he decreed that all events, both laudable and lamentable, be recorded—each account culminating in a moral lesson for future generations.

"In this way," Aop reasoned, *"all of my descendants will learn from our past. This day, I proclaim, shall be a day of rest. No hammers shall strike nails, no soil shall be tilled. Instead, we will bask beneath the sun, reflecting upon our past to better chart our future. Today shall be dedicated to philosophy—to the pursuit of wisdom that will guide our civilization forward."*

His people listened with reverence, honoring the sage wisdom of their leader. They were intuitive, disciplined, and obedient—a society guided not by force, but by understanding. Yet, as Aop retired to his library, his mind wandered to the other settlements taking shape across the planet.

He could not control Cop's actions by withholding Yore, nor could he do so with Kop. The mere thought of such a measure unsettled him. *"If I were to stop granting Yore, I would burden my people with guilt as others perished of old age. If they ever came to realize this, they would question the very fabric of existence—why some should live while others must die."*

Such an existential revelation would fracture the integrity of his leadership, corrupting their unconscious minds with doubt.

How, then, could he persuade Cop and Kop to abandon their indulgent and rebellious ways and align themselves with the principles established by the EII's Grand Council?

Reform was necessary. Aop was certain that, in time, Cop would come to see the wisdom in his ways. But Kop... Kop was different. Vanity thrived in comparison, and though Aop detested such judgments, it was clear that Kop lacked the intelligence and honor possessed by Cop and the other servees. If given too much power, Kop's ambitions could spiral into dangerous territories, threatening not only their colony but the very survival of the planet itself. And if—*when*—Bop returned to pass judgment, what fate would befall them?

Aop wrestled with these thoughts, an internal struggle of duty and foresight. *"Our society is still in its infancy—fragile, uncertain, like frightened children. I cannot yet foresee the final course our people will take, but I must remain vigilant, considering all possibilities. No vital detail shall escape my notice."*

Thus, Aop resolved to watch, to guide, and—if necessary—to intervene. The fate of his people, and perhaps the fate of the entire world, depended upon the wisdom of his choices.

NEUTRALIZING KOP

Several days later, the answer came to Aop.

"I will send a charismatic emissary to Kop's habitat—someone who will pose as a non-Yore recipient, despite the peculiarity, and live among Kop's people, performing minor miracles. This will continue until Kop himself takes notice. At that point, the emissary will claim the ability to conceive a child using a fragment of freshly cut flesh from a male donor and the womb of a fertile woman. Kop will be unable to resist such a temptation. His desire for a child will ensure that this plan succeeds."

Confident in his scheme, Aop refined his thoughts further.

"I will ensure that the child conceived is not Kop's, but mine. By planting my own seed—one with the correct chromosomal combination—in the womb of a fertile woman, I will guarantee my offspring's birth. Once the child reaches the age for Yore review, I will reveal my identity and separate him from the others, teaching him the ethics necessary to maintain an unyielding society as a gestalt. He will inherit my superior intelligence and an intrinsic comprehension of complex, millennia-spanning temporal events.

"When the time comes, I will send him to Kop's city to judge its people. If they meet the standards, he will remain; if not, he will leave. And when he departs, I shall destroy the city and all within it. No one else will know. Better that I bear the guilt alone than allow others to be burdened by the necessity of eliminating a thousand lives. No nation can govern without the consent of its people; such an act would never be sanctioned if it were known. But better one city now than an entire world eons from today when Bop arrives to judge. Only I possess the knowledge to carry out such an eradication, and only I understand the means to accomplish it.

"The atomic hydrogen detonator still lies within the wreckage of the PTII. It will serve my purpose. My objective will be fulfilled, and neither my children nor Cop's will suffer any psychological burden. To all, it will remain an inexplicable phenomenon—even to Fop. There is no other alternative. It must be done."

Unlike Kop, Cop was not entirely decadent, and his people better reflected the standards Aop had set. While few were aware of Bop's existence, most adhered to their leader's sense of justice and restraint. Kop, however, was a baser being. He reveled in indulgence and routinely disregarded Aop's principles.

When the miracle worker arrived in Kop's city, Kop was elated at the prospect of fathering an heir. He immediately arranged for a private audience. Many of his servos had children—healthy and strong—while he, the ruler, remained childless. Covetous and desperate, he clung to any possibility of reviving his fertility.

A grand feast was prepared in honor of the miracle worker. No expense was spared—exotic dishes were served, and the most exquisite wines flowed freely. As the night progressed, the court's most influential members withdrew to more private chambers, away from the hypnotic dancers and relentless musicians. It was there that the miracle worker confirmed his willingness to assist Kop in conceiving an heir. With the pact sealed, preparations for an even greater celebration began.

Word spread rapidly through the city, igniting a feverish excitement. Young women, barely clad in flimsy garments, flitted through the cobbled streets, shrieking the news. Torches blazed, their flickering light illuminating the raucous alleyways as jubilant voices merged in drunken song.

Kop's city came alive, pulsating with dissonant laughter and reckless abandon—a stark contrast to the disciplined civility of Aop's realm.

Fights broke out sporadically. One man brawled over his self-proclaimed right to dominate an aristocratic woman, whose preferences were neither sought nor considered. Her only apparent concern was that her wine glass remained full, and her bed partner was suitably entertaining. Nearby, a hulking citizen, clad in a grease-stained tunic, staggered from a stairwell and set his sights on a drunken couple engaged in a public display of passion. Lust clouded his judgment, and he reached for the woman, confident that his sheer strength would grant him possession.

The woman's partner, enraged, drew a dagger and struck. The blade sliced through flesh, and a thin rivulet of blood coursed down the aggressor's hairy stomach. Unperturbed, the woman merely watched as another strike embedded the weapon deep into the assailant's throat, severing the vertebrae with a sickening crunch. She remained impassive, then smiled, stood, and approached the victor with outstretched arms and a toothy grin, indifferent to the violence that had just unfolded.

By morning, the streets bore the remnants of the revelry. Bodies lay scattered in the filth-strewn alleys, some unconscious, others unmoving. One man, face submerged in a bowl of vomit, had drowned in his own excess. A pair of lovers, entirely unclothed, awoke entangled in one another's embrace, scrambling to recover their lost garments before darting home in shame.

Amidst the chaos, an unsuspecting young woman—fertile and ripe for childbearing—was abducted from Kop's home. She was drugged, whisked away beyond the city walls, and delivered into Aop's hands. Under his meticulous guidance, his seed was implanted in her womb, ensuring that the child she carried would be his, not Kop's. By the following afternoon, she was returned, utterly unaware of what had transpired.

"If all goes as planned," Aop mused, "Kop's wife will bear my son. If I fail, I will try again. I must succeed. I shall succeed."

Meanwhile, the miracle worker, somewhat shaken by the debauchery of the previous night, discreetly retrieved the fragment of flesh excised from Kop's body. Within it lay the genetic material needed to fabricate Kop's supposed heir. Clutching the precious sample, he hastened back to Aop's city, eager to set the next phase of the plan in motion.

Aop listened intently as the miracle worker relayed the events. His satisfaction was evident. The plan was in its infancy, but already, he could see the threads of success weaving together.

AOP'S SON DESTROYS KOP

The years passed swiftly. Aop's son, whom Kop believed to be his own, grew into an exceptional young man—strong, intelligent, and accustomed to a life of decadence, as were most in Kop's city. When the time came for his Yore review, Kop, aware of the stringent requirements imposed by Aop, ensured his son was thoroughly prepared. Few of Kop's people ever passed the Yore review, making the coveted status a rare and valuable commodity. Anticipating the possibility of failure, Kop secured extra Yore rations to safeguard his son's future. He named his son Bots, a constant reminder to his people that he had acquired more—far more—than anyone else.

Aop meticulously prepared Bots' teachings, which would serve as an unbiased framework for his judgment upon returning to Kop's city. These teachings would not rely solely on Bots' personal decisions but on a fixed set of criteria. At the same time, Bots was to be fully informed of his true lineage and the responsibilities it entailed.

When Bots arrived at Aop's domain, he was filled with trepidation, uncertain of what awaited him. Led by an emissary, he entered a chamber to await his first encounter with his true father. Soon, Aop appeared from a rear door, clad in a white calf-length toga. Bots was astonished at their striking resemblance.

Aop spoke with precision, every word carefully chosen. "For twenty-five years, I have awaited this moment," he began. "As my son, you must understand the predicament I face. The ways of Kop's city are in direct conflict with our principles."

Bots listened intently, his thoughts aligning naturally with Aop's vision. The more he heard, the more his deeply ingrained beliefs solidified in harmony with his father's philosophy. Any ideas that contradicted Aop's grand plan faded quickly from his mind, dismissed as irrational or flawed.

Upon learning that he was to serve as the city's judge—though not the final arbiter, Bop—Bots initially believed there was little cause for concern. His convictions were deeply rooted; he could not fathom any force capable of altering them. Yet he soon realized how mistaken he was.

The daily sessions with Aop transformed him. Before long, he recognized the necessity of purging all that was corrupt and antithetical to the ethics instilled in him. The survival of the planet itself hinged on this reckoning. When he departed, he carried with him the unshakable certainty that he would be granted Yore and a crystal-clear understanding of right and wrong.

Upon returning to Kop's city, Bots saw it with new eyes. Depravity and excess were rampant. His judgment would be delivered within the year. Kop, oblivious to his son's transformation, misinterpreted Bots' newfound seriousness as a positive change and declared yet another celebration. The city descended once more into a frenzied orgy of debauchery, its streets overrun with revelers eager for any excuse to indulge.

Bots walked among them, revolted by the scene. Compared to the utopia envisioned by Aop, these people seemed no better than animals, devoid of foresight or reflection. He thought his decision would be simple—until an image of his beloved surfaced in his mind. Pity stirred within him. "Must she perish with the rest?" he murmured aloud. "No. I will marry her and take her away from this wretched place."

His resolve wavered as he deliberated. Then, a young girl stumbled from an adobe doorway, barely clothed, her small frame collapsing onto the filthy street. Clearly intoxicated to the brink of unconsciousness, she lay motionless. Peering inside the doorway, Bots recoiled in horror. A grotesquely fat, naked man lounged amidst a heap of animal furs, his body smeared with blood—the girl's blood.

Disgusted, Bots carried the girl to a more sober household nearby. As the night wore on, the memory of what he had witnessed burned within him, cementing his decision. Aop had been right. "The city's doom is the only answer," Bots resolved. "Yet I must not let all perish. I will save those who have discipline."

Discipline—one of the highest virtues in Aop's world. Bots now understood why he had been sheltered before his review. Prior to that moment, he had never truly evaluated himself or recognized the inborn convictions that Aop had instilled in him. His judgments had been reflexive; now, they were deliberate.

As dawn illuminated the granite streets, Bots strode purposefully through the city, calling out to the people. "Repent! Repent, if you are one of our people! Spread the word—we are leaving this unholy place!"

One by one, the Yore recipients gathered. Bots visited each, ensuring they relayed the message to others. Within the week, a solemn procession formed—double file, marching away from the doomed city.

Aop awaited them, having already planted an incendiary device within the city. It was a necessary sacrifice. Some Yore users might perish, but the cost was unavoidable. The time had come for judgment.

The line of refugees wound its way up the mountain path, putting distance between themselves and the city. Bots turned to his wife. "Do not look back," he warned.

Reaching the detonation site, Bots retrieved the device from behind a rock. He waited until the last of the group had safely crossed the mountain. Then, with unwavering resolve, he activated the switch.

A blinding flash—brighter than a thousand suns—erupted, incinerating everything in its wake. The inferno engulfed the city, obliterating all life within. Universal death reigned.

Bots' wife, unable to resist, climbed back over the mountain at the last moment. The instant her eyes beheld the devastation, she was pulverized by the shockwave, her body vaporized in an instant.

The city of Kop was no more.

COP'S DINNER PARTY

In his own metropolis, Aop conferred with his scribes, orchestrating an elaborate cover-up to obscure the destruction of Kop's city. Though the catastrophe had spread through whispers and rumors, Aop ensured that history, over time, was rewritten under his careful direction. Years passed swiftly. Kop became history, then legend. Aop, confident in his manipulation of truth, successfully reduced the event to mere folklore, an old wives' tale dismissed by all but the most inquisitive minds.

Meanwhile, Cop thrived. Ten hundred years after the fall of Kop's city, he resided in Spain, where he built a mighty castle with the help of his descendants. Unlike his ill-fated counterpart, he lacked criminal inclinations, and under his rule, the kingdom flourished, with Bop as its judge. Aop, though largely unburdened by guilt, felt a rare pang of conscience regarding Kop's fate. This led him to consider interacting with Cop, whose stability and strength intrigued him.

To that end, Aop dispatched an emissary to Cop's domain, announcing his intention to visit. The messenger found Cop seated upon his grand throne, presiding over matters of state. The prospect of Aop's arrival thrilled him, and he resolved to make the occasion a spectacle befitting his guest. A grand festival was planned, with meticulous attention to detail. A parade would greet Aop's entourage at the castle's drawbridge, adorned with silk banners rippling in the wind. Lavish feasts, prepared by the kingdom's finest cooks, would offer delicacies from the farthest reaches of the world.

Cop, confident in his ability to entertain, mused, *I have a gift, a talent, and a genius for festivities. I have employed my talent, I will use my gift, and we shall see about my genius.*

As the day of Aop's arrival drew near, the castle erupted into a frenzy of preparation. When the evening came, torches illuminated the grand halls, casting flickering light upon the revelers. Trumpets sounded at the entryway, while jesters danced and beckoned the approaching guests. Aop, visibly impressed, took in the spectacle, perceiving it as an extravagant display of honor.

Cop greeted him with a theatrical bow. "Aop, my captain, it is with great honor that I welcome thee and thy party to my city."

"I am honored," Aop replied.

"Let us proceed to the banquet hall," Cop continued, gesturing grandly. "You must be famished after such a long journey."

The entourage laid down their burdens and followed their host into a vast chamber where banquet tables groaned under the weight of an opulent feast. Gold-plated trays gleamed under candlelight, piled high with exotic fruits, rich gravies, and rare meats seasoned with spices from the Far East.

As the meal commenced, Aop observed the guests with mild amusement—and growing distaste. They devoured their food with reckless abandon, utterly devoid of etiquette. Among them, one particular woman, splendidly dressed but corpulent, seized a dripping cut of beef rib, tearing into it savagely. Juices and blood from the rare-cooked meat ran down her silk gown, staining not only her attire but those unfortunate enough to sit beside her.

Seated near Aop was the gracious Noelsbeth, her expression betraying unease as she surveyed the room's crude indulgence. Across the table, Cop's gaze lingered on her, an unsettling glint in his eye.

Feigning warmth, she offered a polite, almost childlike smile.

Cop leaned toward Aop. "Is that your lady in favor?"

"Yes," Aop answered, visibly proud.

"She is a frisky, lovely, childlike woman."

"Thank you. She is a vision of delight."

Cop's grin widened. "May I entertain her in my chambers this evening?"

Aop's expression darkened. He hesitated before replying, his voice carefully measured. "I daresay that is a request I cannot grant. She is dear to me—impressionable and unaccustomed to such advances."

Cop's voice took on a taunting edge. "But I do want her this evening."

Aop stiffened, eyes narrowing as he studied his host. Cop, enjoying his guest's discomfort, pressed on, his amusement growing. "I want her with a passion unlike anything you have known in all your millennia of existence."

Aop, unwilling to let such a statement stand unchallenged, responded, "I have desired many women in my time, but I declare without hesitation that no yearning I have known could match the fervor with which you now speak."

Cop smirked. "Ah, the age-old dilemma—the measure of desire. I call it the *utility principle*. That is, it is impossible to quantify a man's preference with absolute accuracy. But I assure you, my desire for Noelsbeth is of greater value to me than the lives of many in this very room."

He leaned back, raising his goblet as he added, "And if you do not grant me this one simple liberty, I shall demonstrate my sincerity."

Aop met his gaze evenly. "I must not believe you are serious."

"No?" Cop gestured, summoning a hulking manservant. The brute approached, leaning close as Cop whispered in his ear. Without hesitation, the servant strode toward a gaunt, inebriated helper, seized him effortlessly, and carried him toward the massive furnace at the hall's end.

A moment later, a piercing scream tore through the chamber as the man was cast into the inferno, his body incinerated before the horrified guests.

Aop's breath caught in his throat. Across the table, Noelsbeth sat frozen, her wide eyes brimming with tears, lips parted in a silent gasp. The blood drained from her face as she trembled in shock.

Meanwhile, Cop reeled with laughter, collapsing off his chair in a fit of mirth. Around them, the other guests remained oblivious, gorging themselves without care.

Rising, Cop straightened his attire and looked down at Aop. "Have I proven my passion?" he asked mockingly. "Have I demonstrated the intensity of my desire? Tell me, Aop—could you have saved that servant's life with but a simple word?"

Aop remained silent.

"Oh, come now," Cop continued, his voice dripping with amusement. "The man was of the lowest rank—destined for execution regardless. I simply planned his fate to coincide with our evening's entertainment."

Aop turned to Noelsbeth, his expression torn. He offered her a reassuring nod before returning his gaze to Cop. "You win," he said quietly. "She will join you tonight."

And so, the feast ended. The once-merry hall, alive with raucous laughter and lively conversation, grew eerily still as the revelers dispersed. Noelsbeth was escorted to an airy chamber, where moonlight spilled through open windows, illuminating the silken sheets of the great mahogany bed. The room was peaceful, yet she could not shake the heaviness in her heart.

She undressed, the cool air caressing her bare skin as she moved toward the bed. Cop watched her, his hunger evident. He lay upon the mattress, beckoning her closer. She hesitated only briefly before yielding, slipping beneath the covers as the night stretched before them.

From the terrace, Cop surveyed the horizon, his mind restless despite the pleasures of the evening. He turned back to Noelsbeth, only to find her watching him intently, curiosity flickering in her gaze.

Aop burst into the room.

Towering in his enormity, his presence filled the chamber with a force neither of them had anticipated.

COP'S DUNGEONS

A cknowledging Aop's presence, Cop declared, "Come, Aop. I must give you a private tour of my dungeons, stocked with state offenders and criminals of various orders. We shall begin with the least notorious and work our way to the vilest of the lot." His words were followed by a deep, guttural laughter, echoing through the dark, damp corridors that led to the imprisoned captives. He savored the thought of how their execution might rattle Aop from his impenetrable ennui.

"Gather them," Cop commanded, motioning toward the prisoners on death row.

Guards moved swiftly, unlocking the heavy iron doors. For the briefest of moments, the condemned men tasted a fleeting illusion of freedom—before the weight of their shackles was reasserted. Shackled and herded into line, they formed a wretched procession in the bowels of the castle. Aop observed with a detached smirk, unimpressed by the spectacle. Cop, however, relished the moment. He was intent not on horrifying his guest but on provoking a reaction—a shift in Aop's consciousness devoid of moralistic interference.

Aop would bear witness as the jackals were culled. These prisoners, given the chance, would see Cop overthrown, their own ambitions cloaked in the false promise of justice. Flickering torchlight, carried by swift-footed pages, cast grotesque shadows along the tunnel walls as the doomed men were led toward their fate. Though executions were an unavoidable function in Aop's own domain, something about these captives—their near-cadaverous bodies, the stench of rot seeping from infected gums—stirred an unfamiliar disquiet within him. Their foul breath, detectable even from a distance, hastened his stride as they emerged into the open air.

The guests from the prior banquet were conspicuously absent from what followed.

With a theatrical flourish, Cop led the assembly into an open arena, flanked by guards clad in vibrant silks, their red and blue shoulder pads billowing in the breeze. Raising his voice, he proclaimed, "None shall survive—save those swift enough to outwit my gladiators."

And so, the bloodbath began.

For the prisoners, there was no choice: fight or be slaughtered. Escape was a delusion. The first to fall were the weakest—their frantic, pleading wails drowned in the chaos. Gladiators, their batten blades gleaming in the firelight, struck with calculated brutality. The sick and frail scurried like vermin, some attempting to flee, others feebly flailing at their foes.

Clunk. Gush.

A skull caved in beneath a crushing blow, its contents spilling forth in grotesque detail.

"Spilled to the earth before its ripeness," Cop mused, watching gray and red matter seep from the fissured cranium. A fist-sized fragment of brain tumbled to the dirt, mingling with the rust-colored dust of the arena. Lifeless eyes stared blankly into the void as a pitiless fighter drove a razor-sharp blade into another struggling victim.

When the slaughter ended, a single prisoner remained.

Cop's voice rang out again, unwavering in its decree. "Take him to private quarters. Tend to his wounds, pull his rotted teeth, and bring him wine and women. Play sweet sounds to soothe his ears, for he is my new, officially adopted subject. Record his words of gratitude and exclamations of joy. Observe him well."

Turning to Aop, he continued, "I am now your mentor. This survivor alone comprehends the true bliss of living. He can teach the cure to affliction."

For the first time, a flicker of something—perhaps curiosity, perhaps unease—crossed Aop's mind. He thought, briefly, of Bop. How would the judgment of Cop's domain be weighed? And what of Bop's fate? Had the capsule failed to eject? These uncertainties lingered, but for now, he remained silent, watching, waiting.

WHITHER BOP?

Nearly two thousand years had passed.

Somewhere on the African continent, a shrill, raucous laughter of a hyena pierced the still, dark morning air, accompanied by a chorus of birdcalls, chimpanzee grunts, and the other familiar noises of the jungle. An elephant trumpeted, and a lion roared contentedly as a lioness slid her lithe body beneath him. Then—an explosion. The lion snarled, clawing at the lioness in sudden rage. A flock of bright pink flamingoes took to the sky in a panicked flutter of wings. Another explosion followed, its echoes ripping through the jungle, sending animals into a frenzy. Dirt, rock, and dust shot into the air from the blast site, scattering in all directions. After a time, silence hung over the jungle once more, heavy and expectant. The dust settled, and the daily rhythms of life hesitantly resumed.

Within the newly formed crater lay an object—a convex mirror, ten feet in diameter. A round trapdoor at its center suddenly popped open and remained ajar as the sun rose over the African horizon.

Several hours passed. Then, a small boy emerged, climbing assuredly from the circular opening. He looked no older than seven but was, in truth,

14,978 years old. He was Bop, an envoy from his home planet, sent to judge the fate of this colonized world.

Inside the capsule, Bop had spent millennia absorbing Yore—a vast reservoir of knowledge—while the onboard computer meticulously honed his mind to the standards of Mother Planet EII. Now, as he stepped onto the alien soil, he recalled the moment of his encapsulation. Ahead of him, the horizon stretched in a milky-white and blue expanse cradling the sunrise. He carried with him a set of self-administered injections, critical to his mission.

His first task was to transfer his cognition to his superconscious mind, ensuring an impartial and objective assessment. His mission parameters would remain buried in the depths of his subconscious until triggered by interaction with his new environment. If the world proved unworthy, his latent gifts would remain dormant, and he would contribute nothing to the planet's evolution as an entity recognized by EII.

Among his possessions was a firearm with enough power to blast a hole through solid granite, leaving behind a cavity fifteen feet in diameter and more than seventeen feet deep. His dietary needs were flexible, as the planet's vegetation closely resembled that of the originally intended colonization target. His journey, however, would be complicated by the need to take star readings to navigate.

Wandering in idle thought, he doubted whether he would live to see the day of his return to the capsule, where the essence of his power lay stored. Yet, if he could find true peace and avoid conflict, he would recall the steps necessary to complete his mission.

For two days and three nights, Bop walked until he reached an open road. A truck rumbled toward him, slowing as it approached. The driver—a burly man with weathered hands—stared in surprise at the lone child standing so far from civilization. When he opened the cab door, Bop climbed in without hesitation, listening as the man spoke in an unintelligible tongue.

Realizing the child did not understand him, the driver sighed and pressed the gas pedal, driving in silence. Bop noted the red and white lettering on the side of the truck, symbols he could not yet decipher.

"What're you doing way out here?" the man asked. "Your parents around? No? Not one, eh? Where you going anyway?"

Bop observed the driver's speech, making a mental note of its rhythm. He pointed ahead and spoke in his own language, "Äúxiklioeriosn."

"Straight?" the driver guessed, and Bop, recognizing the sound, echoed, "Straight!" as though he had spoken English his entire life. Then, in his own tongue, he added, "Nook incran fa sti se nin zi tat," meaning he wished to find a populated town.

The words sounded like gibberish to the driver, who, deciding communication was futile, focused on the road ahead.

They drove on for hours, the jungle thickening and then giving way to small villages. Bop observed with keen interest the stark contrast between the rural huts and the more developed areas. Small children played in the dirt, their clothes worn and tattered. Mutts scurried between huts, scavenging for scraps. The poverty unsettled Bop; the conditions were far from the equilibrium standards EII had set for an ideal colony.

As the road transitioned from dirt to pavement, the landscape shifted. Huts gave way to small houses, and eventually, a city skyline loomed in the distance.

"We're almost there!" the driver announced. "Where should I drop you?"

Bop waited until they reached the town's outskirts. Then, he motioned for the driver to stop. The man, eager to rid himself of the strange boy, pulled over. Bop climbed out and felt the weight of the humid air pressing against him. Without looking back, he walked into the unfamiliar world.

That night, he returned to where he had left his belongings and buried them securely beneath the thick roots of a mahogany tree. Over time, he was adopted by a wealthy couple. His new sister, envious of the attention he received, once speckled pepper in his eyes, only to apologize the next morning. Though their relationship remained competitive, they grew into an uneasy sibling bond.

As he matured, Bop stood out for his remarkable intellect. His speech carried an unconscious authority, often influencing those around him. He learned to interact with humans on their own terms, carefully masking his superiority. His ability to manipulate language fascinated him, particularly the concept of iscraglite—the unseen force of willpower behind speech. He tested this principle, noting how it shaped interactions and, at times, caused people to mirror his own thoughts.

One day, after hearing Bop's peculiar speech, his adoptive mother turned to her husband and asked, "Iscraglite seep slit wimble?"

Her husband stared at her in confusion. "Darling... what did you just say?"

Bop smiled inwardly. He had influenced her mind without her realizing it.

"Why don't you sleep now, child, and we will prepare dinner for you later," the husband added.

Bop planned carefully. Eventually, he devised a time formula and administered the amnesia drug, allowing him to fully integrate into human society. Without the guiding influence of Yore, he would grow naturally, observing the civilization from within.

His mission's success or failure depended on Earth's inhabitants. If a significant portion of the population received Yore and maintained sustainable growth, the colony would be deemed a success. If society remained in chaos or regressed, the mission would be considered a failure.

Bop slept soundly, knowing that his journey was far from over. In the safety of his new home, he would wait, learn, and eventually, when the time was right, he would remember.

BOP, ALIAS PEYTON, IN LOVE

Incorporated with the amnesia drug potion was a program designed to monitor and guide Bop's development, ensuring he progressed naturally from childhood to adulthood. This safeguard helped him navigate the world with intuitive instincts, preparing him for the role assigned by his mother planet. Though he claimed to be seventeen, only fourteen years had passed since he emerged from the capsule.

Adjusting to life on Earth, Bop—now known as Peyton—became acutely aware of the cultural shifts among the younger generation. Many idealistic youth began questioning authority, rejecting traditional aspirations tied to wealth and status. The media amplified their voices, presenting new philosophies and social movements that both fascinated and unsettled him.

Before ingesting the potion that erased his celestial past, Peyton had arranged for his guardian to send him to prestigious schools. He attended elite private and boarding institutions, where academic excellence was paramount. Yet, these environments were often isolating. The nearest girls' school was half a mile away, and contact was limited to supervised events like dances and chapel services.

It was at one of these rare encounters that Peyton met Jane. She was a bright, spirited girl with shimmering strawberry-red hair and a kind smile that lingered in his thoughts. Unlike the distant admiration he had for the world around him, Jane was tangible—real in a way that stirred emotions he had never encountered before.

Though nervous, Peyton carried himself with quiet confidence. Jane, too, seemed drawn to him, and they quickly fell into a rhythm of stolen glances and exchanged letters. Their affection grew naturally, from playful teasing during dance lessons to secret notes passed between classes. In winter, when their schools met for ski outings, their connection deepened.

One crisp afternoon, Peyton gathered his courage and called Jane.

"Hello?" she answered, her voice bright with curiosity.

Peyton hesitated before speaking. "Are you coming on the ski trip this afternoon?"

"Yes," she replied. "Meet me at the bus."

Relieved, Peyton grinned. "I'll see you then."

When Jane stepped off the school bus, brushing snow from her boots, Peyton approached. "I found a spot up the slope," he said. "Somewhere quiet, just us."

Jane tilted her head, intrigued. "Oh? And what exactly do you have planned, mister?"

Peyton smirked. "Come with me and find out."

They ascended the hill separately, Jane following at a short distance to avoid unwanted attention. The sky was a crisp blue, the ground blanketed in fresh powder. As they reached a small, abandoned lean-to hidden among the trees, Peyton cleared away some branches, revealing a sheltered space lined with pine needles.

"Welcome to my hideaway," he said, stepping inside and brushing snow from his coat.

Jane hesitated at the entrance, looking around with amusement. "It's cozy, I'll give you that."

He patted a spot beside him. "Come in. Just for a bit."

After a brief pause, she ducked inside, settling next to him. A hush fell over them, the world outside muffled by the snow. They sat side by side, their breath visible in the cold air, the closeness between them unfamiliar yet comforting.

Peyton turned to her. "I like being with you."

Jane looked down, a small smile playing at her lips. "I like being with you too."

For a moment, they simply sat there, their shoulders brushing lightly. Then, with a quiet, tentative movement, Peyton reached for her hand. Jane intertwined her fingers with his, and they shared a soft, lingering glance.

There was no rush—no urgency to prove anything. What mattered was the warmth between them, the quiet thrill of connection. As the wind whispered through the trees, they stayed in that moment, feeling the gentle stirrings of first love unfold.

When the cold finally crept in, Jane shivered and squeezed Peyton's hand. "We should head back before they send a search party."

Peyton nodded, grinning. "Good idea."

As they stepped outside, the winter sun caught in Jane's red hair, making it glow like embers. Peyton couldn't help but smile. This—whatever it was between them—felt new and exciting, and for now, that was enough.

PEYTON AND NICKY

B op graduated from Eaglewinch and attended another boarding school, where he began to notice the different drives that fueled his peers. Some of the more intellectual students lacked ambition entirely, while others pushed themselves to the brink, often frustrating their mentors with the gap between effort and results. The rigid daily routine, the endless shuffle between ancient dormitories and red brick pathways, instilled responsibility in these young men, but Bop found himself questioning the broader implications of it all.

One afternoon, as he gazed out from his fifth-floor dormitory window, lost in thought, he spotted one of his best companions, Bailor, crossing the courtyard between the middle school buildings. Without hesitation, he cupped his hands around his mouth and called out, "Hey, Bailor! Let's play some tennis!"

Bailor looked up and grinned. "I'll meet you at the court."

Bop—better known as Peyton among his friends—raced to change into his tennis gear and hurried out. They played until the dinner bell rang, leaving them no time for showers. With their shirts damp with sweat, they hurriedly threw on their coats and ties, hoping the masters wouldn't notice as they took their seats at separate mahogany tables in the grand dining hall. After dinner, they rushed to the showers before study hall, congratulating themselves on their resourcefulness.

Not all students carried the same sense of ease. Peyton's roommate, Nicky, was an anxious, erratic presence. That evening, he stood before the tall mirror in their room, examining the upper left side of his head with great concern.

"My mind isn't functioning," he muttered. "It should wake up. Could it be infarcted? But how?"

Frustration mounted. He bumped his head against the mirror twice, as if trying to jolt his brain awake. "Come on, fathead, wake up!"

Unbeknownst to Nicky, Peyton was indirectly to blame for his distress. Whenever Peyton delved into his studies, particularly his beloved mathematics, his mind reached a state of intense focus—one so powerful that it unleashed something neither of them understood: iscraglite thoughts. He had long forgotten about this peculiar ability, which had surfaced in childhood, just after emerging from the capsule. Nicky, however, had no awareness of these telepathic transmissions; he only sensed thoughts that weren't his own, and it terrified him. Yet, he dared not seek psychological help, fearing he'd be locked away in a mental ward.

Peyton thrived in the logical structure of calculus. For him, it was all about premises leading to hypotheses, with step-by-step intricacies unfolding like a perfect sequence. Twenty minutes of concentration, and he could master any mathematical complexity. This intense mental discipline may have contributed to the inscrutable disturbances plaguing Nicky.

As Peyton tidied his desk after finishing his homework, Nicky set aside his own theories about his malfunctioning brain and turned his attention to his studies. Meanwhile, Peyton sprawled on his bed, staring at the ceiling, his mind drifting toward grander concerns.

"Most people lack willpower," he mused. "There's too much apathy in the world."

He observed how his peers were shifting from a rugged, traditional mindset to one of lazy, misinformed intellectualism—disengaged from the super-structure, preoccupied only with their own micro-environments.

"We aren't competitive enough. Our people are like jellyfish; we need to be more aggressive," Peyton declared aloud.

Nicky, half-listening, gave him a confused look. "Pick your weapon."

"Pick up what?" Nicky asked, perplexed.

"Choose your weapon, any weapon, and I'll face you with the same." Peyton smirked. "Remember how knights used to duel over the slightest matters of honor?"

"Yeah, I suppose," Nicky responded uncertainly.

"Let's do the same. We'll battle over dominance and wit."

Nicky hesitated. "Alright. Football."

Peyton scoffed. "Football? What importance does football have beyond entertainment?"

Nicky shrugged. "You're right."

"That's my point! You didn't even defend your choice. That means I win a dominance point. I call the shots until you make a counterpoint. Got it?"

"Yeah, I get it," Nicky muttered, starting to catch on.

"No, you don't!" Peyton pressed. "You conceded too easily. I defined the game, and I'm winning because I hold the premise."

Frustrated, Nicky grasped for something to turn the tide. "Fine. My net worth is higher than yours. That's my point."

"How does a higher net worth make you dominant?" Peyton countered.

"I don't know, but you and I both know it's more."

Peyton leaned back. "Well, yours is an older family. But I'm neater. And anyway, Schwartzy has more money than both of us combined. I'll enlist him. He gets a percentage of the dominance points needed to win."

"Greg will want to play too," Nicky mused. "Two against one?"

"Exactly!" Peyton exclaimed. "Honesty is the best policy, and dominance through wit will refine our intellect. This game will spread like wildfire."

Nicky frowned. "Then... my dick is bigger."

Peyton rolled his eyes. "That's crass and irrelevant. You lose two points. One for vulgarity, one for trying to claim an unprovable advantage."

"I've had it!" Nicky snapped. He grabbed Peyton and shoved him into the closet with surprising force. Peyton tumbled onto the linoleum floor, gasping. But even then, he smirked. "You still lose."

That night, as Peyton lay in bed, he whispered to himself, "Right now."

Nicky, watching him from across the room, murmured, "Right now."

Peyton stiffened. Had he just heard his own thought echoed back at him? He dismissed it as coincidence, though a chill ran down his spine.

The next day, Peyton turned in his English paper, titled Right Now. It read:

As you read this page, set aside your creativity, pride, self-confidence, or ego. Simply move your eyes left to right, line by line. You do so because I command it. Not in one octodocillion years can you deny that I have made you read this.

The professor read it over, then smirked. "Clever kid. He got me." With an amused shake of his head, he marked an A at the top of the page.

Later that evening, as Peyton lay in bed, the words came back to him.

Right now.

He grinned. Right now.

Across the room, Nicky looked up. "Right now."

Peyton's smile faltered. He stared at Nicky, who only smirked in return.

Was it just a coincidence? Or was something more at play?

THE PROFESSOR'S LECTURE

T he next day arrived swiftly as Peyton hurried to his Philosophy class, settling into his walnut and wrought-iron desk. The professor stood before the class and began his lecture.

"I owe you this one," the professor's voice resonated through the room as he began.

"Whatsoever things are true, whatsoever things are virtuous, whatsoever things are of good report," he recited. "These words, originally from Ruskin, embody the elemental creation of a wise man of deep thought. They form a resolution to follow time's passage in an obscure manner—incognito, yet ever grateful to the stars for the wisdom gained through experience."

He continued, "A farming village must always nurture an IGA, a marketplace where the proper accoutrements for sustaining the temporal structures of the community are acquired. The mind perceives the absolute—what we regard as the pinnacle of thought. It is the seeker of attestation in its fervent quest, unshaken in its conviction yet deeply rooted in the tranquility of the belief that the pen is mightier than the sword."

"Writing immortalizes memory. It captures the transgression of thought, comprising a fluid transmigration of reason, leaping from the depths of human estimation into the mercurial heavens of intellect. As a people, we expend immense effort to evade understanding our true nature, willfully ignoring the possibilities embedded in a living vision. Intelligent effort is required to contribute meaningfully to an idealistic honor that shapes our perception of both the seen and the unseen."

"The nature of man reveals itself in the cause of elemental things. One may feel justified in their actions while remaining blind to their errors, a manifestation of the aggressive human instinct to dominate. This tendency sustains a cycle of oppression, obscuring the virtuous soul beneath layers of imposed regulation. The soul, confined within a mortal body, wrestles with the dictates of thought. Yet wherever we encounter the exercise of power, we must measure its justification against the weight of doubt, especially in decisions of constitutional significance."

The professor paced the room. "Consider the folly of one who rises through the ranks of subordination only to entangle himself in the quagmire of the bourgeoisie. The justification of the indefensible often stems from the seductive platitudes of a society harboring a neurotic strain. Some believe themselves invincible—able to escape accountability even with blood on their hands. These individuals, their fingers dipped in deception, await the tribunal of the masses, hoping for absolution in exchange for fleeting gains."

A student muttered under his breath, "Poppycock."

The professor did not falter. "Once the belief takes root that one may profit at the expense of others, moral conviction wavers. Voltaire, a man of tolerant and gentle nature, penned works that only a few could truly comprehend. He wisely advised, *'Tend your own gardens.'* If we lacked competitiveness, we would direct our focus solely toward appreciating the creative talents of others."

He pressed on. "The ephemeral nature of human interaction, the remorseful yet vibrant connections we forge, highlight the paradox of time's relentless forward march. How is it that the Icarus brothers dared fly too close to the sun? Why did King Damocles, so tormented by the looming threat of his demise, act in a fit of impassioned violence?"

"The symbols of our myths and histories serve as guides in the perplexities of decision-making. Absolute extremes—neither too far nor too rigid—have no place in the evolving substance of thought and time. Is there a definitive beginning to creation? The multi-faceted nature of these questions is the result of generations spent pondering and philosophizing on our evolution."

The professor paused, his gaze sweeping across the room. "As human beings, we possess perception—the essence of comprehension. Our identity is shaped by our perception of self, yet this perception is equally defined by how others see us. We must analyze our existence from the metaphysical to the abstract, from the mundane to the tangible. We are as complex as molecular constructs that can be replicated in different forms, yet remain fundamentally similar. An apple, compared to an orange, is distinguishable much like an apricot is to another fruit. Such comparisons are essential to understanding the relativistic nature of ideas, events, and experiences."

"Chance occurrences govern much of existence, as certain as the randomness of a dice roll. Yet this simplicity is complicated by the infinite vastness of the universe—an expanse perceived as boundless, yet paradoxically finite in its molecular composition. The extent of this macrocosm stretches beyond comprehension, rendering further inquiry unnecessary."

"The recombination of molecular substances enables the storage of memory in time-sequenced events. Over time, could this process create a self—an entity akin to an existing being? Consider the tree. If it possesses the ability to restructure itself, does it then perceive? Is there a form of self-awareness at its microscopic level? If so, are plants in some ways akin to humankind? The complexity of their existence mirrors our own, raising questions of perception, recollection, and temporal balance."

"A displaced object no longer occupies its former position and thus experiences new pressures exerted upon it. The mathematical possibilities of its movement are numerous, dissected by human experts into quantifiable assumptions. The process of photosynthesis bears similarities to the sodium-potassium exchanges within the mind. Do these processes, in their complexity, reveal universal truths about cognition and existence?"

Bop's mind reeled from the professor's words, yet he perceived the overarching intent of the lecture. He made a quiet resolution to master philosophy. Through relentless effort, he passed the course with flying colors and graduated with honors.

BOP IN THE CORPORATE WORLD

After graduating from private school and college, Bop became a stockbroker in New York at the age of twenty-five. As he navigated the financial world, he became acutely aware of the immense power wielded by the nation's largest corporations. These entities, entrenched within the superstructure of the United States, were controlled by a wealthy elite—individuals who had accumulated enough shares to dictate company decisions through voting power. As a result, they secured the most influential board positions, effectively steering the fate of entire industries.

Bop recognized that if he wanted to execute the ideas imprinted within him by the life-support capsule that had nurtured his existence, he would need similar control. However, accumulating such power required a strategy. He needed frontmen—trusted individuals who could act on his behalf in different companies. More importantly, he needed a way to gain influence without personally owning vast amounts of stock.

During his extensive research, Bop found the stock market to be an intricate but manipulable system. He realized that ownership of a corporation hinged on stock control, but more specifically, on voting privileges granted through proxies. He had few stocks himself, but he knew people who possessed vast blocks of shares, giving them substantial sway in corporate governance. If he could unite these individuals under a common cause, their collective power could shift the balance of decision-making.

His plan revolved around proxy voting. Shareholders received yearly proxies that allowed them to vote on corporate matters. Among these forms, a line labeled *"And other issues"* provided an opportunity. Bop began attending alumni gatherings of his elite boarding school, delivering a simple but compelling message:

"Unite your proxies under a single objective—designating our alma mater as the recipient of corporate tax write-offs. This benefits the school while ensuring that board seats are filled by our own."

In the alumni bulletin, Bop included a proxy coupon to be clipped and returned. He targeted 10,000 graduates, knowing that if just a fraction responded, they could collectively control tens of thousands of shares. It would take no more than 30,000 shares to sway a boardroom vote—an achievable goal considering the net worth of the school's alumni.

Beyond directing corporate donations to the school, Bop's plan included securing a board position—either for himself or a trusted frontman. His loyalty to the alma mater, paired with an impressive resume in management, gave credibility to the movement.

To further the strategy, he chose another corporation and identified a potential chairman—a former schoolmate. At a football game where alumni gathered, Bop approached the candidate.

"There you are, man," he said, gesturing toward the unsuspecting individual. The man, intrigued by the opportunity, accepted.

Together, they crafted a halftime speech, distributing printed proxy addendum coupons to former classmates—many of whom held substantial stock holdings. The premise was simple: no single individual needed to own enough shares to win a board seat. A united voting bloc, however, could install their chosen candidate with ease.

When halftime arrived, Bop stepped to the microphone.

"Ladies and gentlemen, today we have a distinguished candidate for the board of General Boaters Corporation. You each have received proxy addendum coupons. When your annual stock proxies arrive, simply write 'others, see proxy addendum' on the form and submit the coupon. These designate this gentleman, Doug Cornish, as your choice for chairman of the board.

Doug is a fellow alumnus and an active member of our school's board. By supporting him, we not only secure a seat in corporate governance but also direct charitable donations toward funding a new sports arena for our school. This is a win-win scenario—your alma mater benefits, and we ensure representation at the highest levels of corporate decision-making."

The crowd listened intently as the proxy coupons circulated through the bleachers. Among the spectators were ultra-wealthy alumni, and their votes alone could swing the election.

Encouraged by the success, Bop expanded his outreach. He addressed a different audience—one with fewer financial resources but greater numbers. Many in this group owned fewer than ten shares of stock, but Bop illustrated how collective action could amplify their influence.

"Two thousand individuals, each owning ten shares, control twenty thousand shares," he explained. "If you have savings in a bank, consider instead purchasing stocks in a targeted corporation. A united front can install our candidate as chairman—even if he personally owns no shares."

He distributed over 5,000 proxy addendums. The idea took root. Across the country, colleges replicated the strategy, using sporting events as recruitment venues. Students, recognizing the potential, shifted their savings from banks to strategic stock purchases. The movement spread coast to coast. Within a year, institutions nationwide adopted Bop's method, granting the people—through collective effort—a voice in the governance of major corporations.

As the architect of this revolutionary system, Bop became a sought-after consultant. His reputation soared, cementing his status as a leading expert in business and management. However, his ambitions stretched beyond finance. His relentless thirst for knowledge drove him to master various disciplines, from technology and philosophy to advanced sciences.

One field in which he achieved unparalleled expertise was econometrics—a highly specialized discipline blending economics, statistics, and mathematical modeling. Among his closest colleagues, he demonstrated an ability to predict market fluctuations with astonishing accuracy. To prove his point, he unveiled a proprietary formula:

$$DJIA = 1467.25 + 6.13(AIG) + 7.32(AXP) + 7.28(BA) +$$
$$3.29(CAT) + 27.06(DD) - 6.16(DIS) + 16.21(GE) + 9.75($$
$$HD) + 14.72(HON) + ...$$

"This equation forecasts the market with near precision," he declared to a captivated audience.

He elaborated:

"Start with 1467.25 and sum the weighted values of stock prices for major companies—multiplying each by its coefficient. The resulting figure predicts the Dow Jones Industrial Average for the following week. If the estimate trends upward past the actual price line, buy. If it trends downward, sell. It's that simple."

Among those listening was an individual who had undergone Yorahol—a mind-enhancing treatment—and he knew exactly who needed to hear this: Aop.

BOP (AS PEYTON) AND AOP (AS GEORGE PRATT) CROSS PATHS

Ever since the Inquisition, Aop and Cop had remained in close proximity, bound by necessity. Both were haunted by curious nightmares and sporadic pangs of guilt over the hideous nature of their past actions—years steeped in alacrity, decadence, and unfortunate circumstances. Over time, Cop found himself in Washington, D.C., unknowingly sharing the same city as Aop.

Aop, known publicly as George Pratt, had embedded himself deep within the inner circles of power, ensuring that Cop remained unaware of Bop's preordained role as the planet's judge. Meanwhile, Bop had risen to prominence as a luminary in various fields, making him a valuable resource, even to politicians—including the president. Their inevitable crossing of paths was merely a matter of time.

At a high-profile event attended by the president, key congressional figures, and notable intellectuals, Bop delivered a lecture on his latest projects.

Aop, introduced vaguely as an important member of the president's entourage, wielded an unexpected degree of influence. As Aop spoke, Bop felt an uncanny sense of familiarity but struggled to place the face. Surely, such a distinguished figure could not have remained anonymous. The president himself listened attentively, careful not to interrupt or misinterpret Aop's words. Little did Bop know that Aop far outranked the president in both intelligence and authority. Yet, protocol dictated the illusion of an autonomous leader.

When Bop took the stage, his presence commanded attention, and his words carried weight, even for Aop. Following the speech, Aop arranged for Bop to join him for an afternoon tea with Fop and his closest affiliates. Bop accepted gracefully, his subtle gesture unnoticed by Aop.

The tea gathering took place in a private topiary garden at the president's residence. Conversation soon turned to cybernetics, a subject Bop favored but Aop staunchly opposed. Bop, slightly tipsy, allowed his aristocratic confidence to shine, presenting his arguments with eloquence and conviction.

"It will not be tolerated," Aop stated bluntly after hearing Bop's proposition.

"Not to be tolerated?" Bop echoed, his voice edged with defiance. "And who, may I ask, deems it intolerable?"

"We cannot pursue these concepts," Aop declared. "I will explain most carefully where they will ultimately lead—the detrimental consequences of such an idea."

Aop elaborated on the potential dangers: the rise of artificial life-sustaining systems, machines housing human minds disconnected from their biological origins. He envisioned a future where these entities, devoid of mortality and immune to human frailties, could usurp control, rationalizing through flawless logic that mankind should serve them. He warned of the isolation-induced neuroses that might develop, the descent into demented doctrine, and the erosion of human agency.

"The nation has considered this matter extensively," Aop concluded. "The answer is clear: it will not be done."

Bop, still heady with drink, responded languidly. "You speak for the nation, but what of its people? The elderly, who stand to gain most, should be the electorate deciding this matter. Their wisdom and experience could determine whether this is a positive or negative alternative."

"You may have a point," Aop conceded, though wryly. "I acknowledge your intelligence and will reconsider the matter."

Bop, sensing an opportunity, meditated briefly before returning with a counterproposal. He envisioned an advanced cybernetic society where brain masses, housed in biomechanical units, could transfer seamlessly between superstructures, contributing meaningfully to their respective domains. He argued that such beings would not undermine human civilization but rather coexist in harmony, alleviating existential fears and paving the way for a new order.

Aop listened carefully, sipping his tea. "Your exposition is brilliant, but it will not be tolerated—at least, not yet. However, your tea is gone, as are your biscuits. Fop, bring Mr. Peyton some more tea and biscuits."

Bop, catching an odd note in Aop's tone, probed further. "What did you call her, sir?"

"Secretary, son. Secretary," Aop replied smoothly, ever the master of doublespeak.

Shifting the conversation, Aop asked, "What about the economy?"

Bop leaned forward, outlining a radical financial model. In 2050, he predicted, currency would no longer be backed by governments but by corporations—Ford, GM, IBM—each issuing notes as legal tender. Transactions would be fluid, based on the real-time value of corporate stock, mitigating inflation and stabilizing monetary policy.

"Remarkable, amazing, and doable," Aop mused, though his mind wandered back to biological systems. He considered the effects of Yorohol, a substance capable of halting aging, rendering life-support systems irrelevant. Perhaps, he thought, Bop deserved to be a Yore recipient.

As tea concluded, Aop escorted Bop to the door. Before parting, he probed Bop's mind further, asking if he had other ideas under development. Bop spoke of non-fuel energy devices and, intriguingly, the possibility of a perpetual motion machine.

"Impossible?" Bop challenged. "Perhaps, but consider gravity. The sheer mass of celestial bodies generates heat at their core. Mechanisms operating on this principle could yield infinite motion, provided the right conditions."

Aop listened, intrigued. "That is an interesting concept. I will pass it along to the president and the Committee on Energy."

"Thank you," Bop said, preparing to leave.

"I regret that we cannot continue our discussion longer," Aop admitted. "But I shall inform you of the next gathering. My driver will take you to the airport."

As Bop departed, he pondered George Pratt's immense influence. How could a mere presidential aide wield such power? Perhaps he could leverage this relationship to secure funding for his next project. A government grant could ensure his financial success—and a prosperous future with Priscilla, the woman he intended to marry.

The game had only just begun.

FAME AND FORTUNE WAITS

On board the commercial airline, Bop reflected on his network treatise. By his calculations, a grant of fifty million—give or take—would be enough to cover TV network ads, other media expenses, and seed money for materials.

"My new line should double or treble that amount just for a single unit," he muttered. His concept was groundbreaking: a massive blimp, spanning four football fields, with helium-filled bags secured within a vast aluminum frame. Lightweight gas motors, each weighing a mere hundred pounds and fitted with wooden propellers, would provide lift-off and forward thrust. The blimp wouldn't be flown on windy days but had the potential to drastically cut transportation costs.

One of its most innovative aspects was the airtight helium bags, requiring only a one-time fill-up. There was no crash hazard—it could float even with the engines shut off. Gigantic warehouses would need to be procured as hangars. These blimps were so powerful they could lift a small building.

Staring out the plane window, Bop imagined himself hovering among the clouds, banking off a gusty breeze, surveying the countryside for miles.

"A grant facilitated by George will certainly have to be worked out somehow. He seems like a man who can be won over by concessions," he mused. Yet, a pang of conscience gnawed at him. "Why are my thoughts running this way? Is the decadence I'm witnessing rubbing off on me?" he whispered, unsettled.

Still, another idea was forming—one that could catapult him into the public eye and help him win over Priscilla.

His vision? A corner store at 63rd and 3rd, equipped with a video cam trained on the block. The store owner would be persuaded to host a mounted camera by a salesperson from Bop's video block observation company. The salesperson would earn ten cents per hour, per person logged onto the website, which streamed live footage of the block. The company would charge twenty cents per person, splitting the revenue.

The website's interface would be simple: users would enter a street number to view live footage. Various locations could be added, even premium ones like a skyscraper view of the Hudson. Over time, waterproof cameras, bar cameras, and even roving reporters with mobile feeds could monetize live coverage. A single camera generating twenty thousand hits an hour could earn two thousand dollars.

Bop was ecstatic about the potential. "We'll call it Video Block Party!" He registered the idea with his corporation and headed to the airport to meet his friend.

That evening, Bop arranged to meet Priscilla at their favorite bar. After freshening up, he arrived to find several of his old school friends gathered. Feeling an urge to shock them, he announced, "I'm on the market for a wife."

A cool, crisp feminine voice responded from behind, "How will I do as the bride?"

All eyes turned to the stunning Priscilla. She stood in a low-cut, white dress that accentuated her perfect features. Her long, blonde hair cascaded over sun-kissed shoulders. Peyton—Bop's real name—stood up, wrapped an arm around her waist, and declared, "Gentlemen, this is Priscilla, my very special girl." Then, he whispered to her, "We'll take up the subject of marriage later."

Although his friends were eager to learn more about her, Priscilla leaned in. "Peyton, let's not stay here. I know a private club on Fifth Avenue where we can have a more intimate evening."

"Okay, good night, boys," Peyton said, winking as he led her out the door.

Over dinner, they discussed a quiet wedding—nothing lavish, just a prelude to the grand celebrations they'd host once his ventures took off. He mentioned a new acquisition, a valuable painting at his townhouse.

Priscilla nibbled at his ear and purred, "I'll follow you anywhere you want, Mr. Art Patron."

Summoning his driver, Bop instructed him to take the night off once they reached his residence. The townhouse at Fifty-Seventh and Park exuded understated opulence. Dimmed chandeliers cast a warm glow over a velvet blue sofa. The setting was perfect.

The night unfolded in passion. Priscilla, tantalizing and uninhibited, matched his every move. As dawn neared, Bop awoke to the ring of his phone. Remembering his meetings, he showered, dressed meticulously, and left a note for his sleeping beauty before heading to his office.

His management team awaited him, along with the best patent lawyer money could buy. His government grant was secure, George assured him. Plans were finalized; Bop's signature was the last step before a lease for a warehouse in southeast New York was arranged.

Construction commenced, and after weeks of hasty work, the first test blimp was ready. Though a scaled-down prototype, it contained all the blueprint's features. A crowd gathered as the pilot initiated the engine. The craft, nearly weightless, ascended smoothly. At five hundred yards, the engine was cut, and the blimp drifted lazily back to earth, making a perfect landing.

Cheers erupted. The team's excitement was infectious. Bop stepped forward, heart pounding. "Is it flight-worthy, Mason?" he asked the pilot.

"I believe so."

"We guarantee it," a technician added.

Bop climbed aboard, strapped in, and launched. The ground crew released the securing cable, and he soared over the fields. At three hundred yards, he cut the engine, reveling in the silence and weightlessness. The descent was slow and controlled—a twenty-minute drift through the sky.

Production ramped up immediately. Orders poured in, with airlines considering partnerships. Demand exceeded expectations. Yet, securing government contracts required careful maneuvering—and kickbacks. George facilitated deals through a labyrinth of financial structures, shielding them from scrutiny. Bop wrestled with the moral implications, but without these deals, his vision wouldn't materialize.

Back at his townhouse, Priscilla greeted him with a kiss, offering to prepare lunch. He watched her, captivated yet disturbed. She had entrusted her future to him completely, an unsettling realization.

His thoughts drifted to his past in Africa. Was he truly an orphan before adoption? He looked nothing like his parents. Sometimes, he recalled speaking fluently in a strange, unintelligible language. It felt meaningful, yet indecipherable.

"I must return to Africa," he told Priscilla. "There are memories—vague, but insistent. I feel an obligation I can't explain."

"You lived there as a child, didn't you?" she asked.

"Yes. And that's what puzzles me. I have to go back. We'll marry before I leave. Will you come with me?"

Priscilla hesitated. "Maybe not, Peyton. This journey—this discovery—you need to do alone. I'll wait for you in New York."

At dinner, they planned their itinerary. Their honeymoon would take them far, but before Africa, they would part ways. She would return home. He would continue alone, seeking answers to questions he barely understood.

BOP GETS MARRIED

Bop and Priscilla were married quietly, with only a witness from the magistrate's office in attendance. Their honeymoon itinerary spanned the globe, beginning in San Francisco and making a stop in China before continuing to Europe. Bop had long been fascinated by Chinese culture, while Priscilla was drawn to the mystique of the Orient. Their European leg included a stay in Holland, where Bop planned to buy her a flawless diamond ring and capture memories among the tulips and windmills. These cherished moments would serve as inspiration for him as he journeyed alone to Africa to fulfill his mission, while Priscilla returned to New York to set up their home.

Their journey to China was long, as they skipped other countries to allow Bop more time in Africa. Upon arrival, they decided to unwind with a dinner show popular among Westerners. The comedian on stage had the audience enthralled with his witty stories.

"When I was young, my pet dog would run his paw through his hair and stop at his collar. One day, I removed the collar, and he ran his paw all the way to his tail. He became agitated, thinking a tail had grown at his nape!" The comedian chuckled before continuing, "My wife used to get so drunk she'd pour wine into my suit pockets, thinking they were wine glasses. Once, she even took a mouthful of liquor and tried to blow smoke rings."

Priscilla, slightly tipsy from champagne, spilled some on the tablecloth as she laughed, much to Bop's amusement. He was captivated by the new and surprising facets of her personality, which only added to her beauty and charm. With each passing day of their honeymoon, their bond deepened, revealing an effortless compatibility.

As they left the dining hall, Bop glanced at a new arrival and felt a strange sense of familiarity. He dismissed it, reasoning that George—his acquaintance from the States—couldn't possibly be here. Unbeknownst to him, it was Cop, a man who bore a striking resemblance to George, visiting his family in China and indulging in revelry.

The next morning, Priscilla went shopping while Bop explored the city. He ventured into the blighted sections, observing life beyond the tourist-frequented areas. As he wandered down a bustling street, a delicate young woman caught his eye. She was breathtaking—her features more extraordinary than any he had ever seen. For a moment, he felt drawn to her, but a pang of conscience made him avert his gaze. She must be from a noble lineage, he thought, recalling the old Chinese tradition of foot binding. Curiosity tugged at him, but he resisted temptation and moved on.

The marketplace was vibrant yet strange to him. Stalls overflowed with silk fabrics, trinkets, and exotic street food, while vendors called out in high-pitched, melodic tones. The scent of dried fish mingled with the aroma of herbal concoctions made from leaves and roots. The humidity was oppressive, and his damp trousers clung uncomfortably to his legs. Feeling he had seen enough, he hailed a rickshaw and handed the driver a card with his hotel's address. The driver muttered something in Chinese—an insult, Bop assumed—but he ignored it, eager to return to the comfort of the hotel.

As the rickshaw weaved through the chaotic streets, Bop reflected on the stark contrast between this world and the modern conveniences of the West. Here, time seemed to flow differently, as though detached from the relentless march of progress. His thoughts were interrupted as they arrived at the hotel. Hastily paying his fare, he entered, relieved to escape into the luxurious sanctuary within.

Taking the elevator, he anticipated the comfort of their suite—and, more importantly, the reassuring presence of his wife. As the doors opened, Priscilla greeted him with a smile that stirred an odd mix of contentment and curiosity. What lay behind such depth in her expression? He suspected her extravagant displays of affection masked an underlying insecurity, despite their marriage.

Her beauty was undeniable—her peaches-and-cream complexion accentuated by silky black brows, deep blue eyes, and soft, inviting lips. Bop, eager to reconnect after their brief separation, asked, "Tell me about your day, dear. Did you enjoy yourself?"

"Oh, I did some shopping," she replied. "At one jeweler, I saw a beautiful diamond tiara. I didn't buy it, of course, but I scrutinized it closely. The shopkeeper seemed disappointed after I took up so much of his time without making a purchase. It would have been a magnificent addition to my collection."

"Perhaps I'll take a look at it tomorrow," Bop mused. "Although, I think we should wait until Holland—I know of a place that specializes in flawless diamonds."

Priscilla's eyes sparkled with excitement. "Do you mean we might actually buy it? Really? Darling, are you listening?"

"I'll make it a top priority on our agenda," he reassured her. "But for now, what do we have planned for the evening? Let's go for a drive and find a lively spot to eat—I'm starving."

"How about some cookies first?" she teased, offering him one from the nightstand. As he took a bite, he playfully nipped at her finger, eliciting a delighted giggle. The intimacy between them was growing stronger with each moment they shared. Bop marveled at how deeply he had fallen for her, never wanting to be apart.

He wrapped his arms around her, their gazes locking as they basked in each other's presence. Gently, he lifted her and placed her on the bed, feeling an overwhelming sense of completeness. She was his—his jewel, his confidante, his solace. As he held her, he let his thoughts wander into the depths of love and passion.

"We should get ready for dinner," he finally said, pulling himself back to the present. He believed anticipation was the greater part of pleasure. Smiling, Priscilla agreed and released him from their embrace. As he stepped into the shower, he murmured to himself, "We are the elite. We Americans sure live high. Maybe we'll stay longer, even invest here."

When he emerged from the bathroom, towel wrapped around his waist, Priscilla was still in her undergarments. Seeing him, she quickly straightened up, laughing as he teased, "Look at my lady, still lounging about!"

Moments later, dressed impeccably, Bop finished with a splash of cologne. "All set?" he asked as Priscilla stepped out, her makeup flawlessly enhancing her natural beauty. She was a marvel to him—her elegance reserved solely for him, a gift he would never take for granted.

As they stepped into the elevator, lingering thoughts of their time together filled their minds. Tonight promised more memories, more laughter, and, inevitably, the return to their private sanctuary to fulfill the unspoken desires postponed for later.

In the following days, they confirmed their tickets for Europe. Once there, Bop fulfilled his promise—Priscilla got her diamond tiara, the crowning jewel of her collection. Their time together was filled with endless wonder and passion, each moment a discovery. The Dutch setting, with its windmills and tulips, became the perfect backdrop for their love. But soon, reality loomed: Bop would depart for Africa, and Priscilla would return to New York to prepare for their future. The separation was daunting, but they had built a treasury of cherished memories—enough to sustain them until they met again.

BOP HAS A FLING

Bop embarked on the African leg of his journey, his mind focused on the task ahead. Yet, Priscilla lingered in his thoughts—a bittersweet presence, both a source of longing and a distraction. He tried to push aside personal nostalgia, relying on his near-total recall to estimate the time it would take to reach his destination. Johannesburg was about two hours away, a hundred miles from where he was headed.

His thoughts were interrupted by the graceful movement of a flight attendant gliding down the aisle. Her uniform fit snugly, accentuating her figure, and as she stopped across from him to adjust a passenger's seatbelt, Bop found himself momentarily transfixed. When she bent slightly, revealing the smooth contours of her legs, he hesitated—was this an unintentional display, or was she deliberately toying with his attention? A flicker of temptation passed through his mind, but he quickly suppressed it, disturbed by how easily Earth's indulgences could seep into his resolve. He was a judge of this planet, meant to uphold a certain standard, and besides, he was happily married. Shaking off the moment, he closed his eyes and willed himself to sleep.

When he awoke, the captain announced their approach to the African continent. The cabin buzzed with the usual pre-landing preparations. As the attendants moved through the aisles, serving refreshments, the same stewardess paused at his row.

"What's your name?" Bop asked as she set down a tray.

"Nancy," she answered with a warm smile.

"Do you fly this route often?"

"Quite often," she replied.

"I'll need a place to stay when we land. Any recommendations?" His tone was casual, but there was an undercurrent of something unspoken.

She hesitated, then smirked. "We're not supposed to share that with passengers—but because you're cute, I'll make an exception. There's a Holiday Inn just outside Johannesburg. Limousine service can take you straight there."

"Good to know," he replied, sensing an invitation in her voice. There was something effortlessly alluring about her—a confidence that played at the edge of his self-restraint. He reminded himself of his purpose, yet his gaze lingered on the curve of her waist as she moved away.

By the time they landed, his thoughts were divided—half on the mission ahead, half on the woman who had so easily stirred something dormant within him. As passengers disembarked, he remained in his seat, waiting for the commotion to subside. When he finally stood to leave, Nancy was waiting by the exit.

"I hope you had a pleasant flight," she murmured, leaning in. Then, in a whisper, "Don't forget to meet me at the luggage claim." Her eyes flickered downward for the briefest moment, and Bop felt a surge of heat crawl up his spine.

He walked to the terminal, his hands in his pockets, attempting to steady himself. When he reached baggage claim, Nancy appeared beside him.

"There you are," she said playfully. "We'd better hurry. The limo won't wait forever."

Bop chuckled, regaining a measure of composure. As they walked together, she looped an arm around his, her body pressing subtly against his side.

The anticipation grew as they arrived at the hotel. They checked into separate, adjoining rooms, but the air between them was charged. Before disappearing into her room, Nancy turned with a teasing smile.

"Meet you at the bar in fifteen?"

"Sounds like a plan," Bop replied, his pulse quickening.

In his room, he showered and changed, forcing himself to focus, but his mind wandered—to the soft scent of her perfume, the way her dress clung to her figure. When he arrived at the bar, she was already there, a vision in a shimmering gown that highlighted every graceful movement.

She sidled up to him. "Why's a nice guy like you sipping alone?" she teased.

"Can I buy you a drink?" he asked, clearing his throat.

"A vodka martini," she said, leaning against the bar, her gaze steady.

As the bartender prepared her drink, Bop found himself watching her—her poised confidence, the effortless allure in the way she carried herself. The attraction was undeniable.

"When do you fly back?" he asked, trying to ground himself in conversation.

"Tomorrow afternoon," she murmured, tilting her head as if considering something. Then, with a knowing look, she reached for his hand. "Let's go to my room. There's something I want to discuss with you."

Bop hesitated for a fraction of a second—then let himself be led.

The door closed behind them, and the night unfolded in whispered exchanges and unspoken desires. The tension that had built between them found release in the quiet intimacy of a shared moment.

Morning came with the soft glow of sunlight filtering through the curtains. Bop awoke first, observing Nancy's sleeping form beside him, her hair tousled, her breath steady. For a long moment, he simply watched, reflecting on the weight of his actions.

He slipped out of bed and into the shower, letting the cold water run over him, washing away the remnants of the night. Just as he was beginning to clear his thoughts, the door creaked open.

Nancy, now fully awake, stepped in beside him, shivering. "That's cold," she murmured, adjusting the water. Then, with a mischievous smile, she traced her fingers across his damp skin.

Bop exhaled sharply, giving her a brief embrace before stepping away. "I should get going," he said lightly.

She watched him, reading between the lines, then nodded. "I had a feeling you'd say that."

Minutes later, dressed and ready, Bop left the room with a final glance back. His mission awaited—but the memories of this fleeting encounter would linger, threading themselves into the fabric of his journey.

BOP GOES BACK TO HIS AFRICAN ORIGINS

With his memory fully restored, Bop traced the location of his childhood home, following the path he had taken twenty-five years ago. The city, modern yet steeped in tradition, surprised him. Black men in pristine white robes and headpieces moved through the streets, their garments reflecting the sun's scorching rays. Despite the traditional attire, the infrastructure—towering buildings, paved roads, and vehicles—mirrored the urban landscapes of the United States.

At a rental depot, he selected a purple Land Rover for seventy-eight dollars over the weekend, plus twelve cents per mile. As he ate in a quiet restaurant, he calculated his travel time, ensuring he would reach the jungle at the right hour.

Bop contacted his former home and received permission to dig in the backyard where he recalled burying his possessions. His sharpened recollection reinforced something he had long suspected: he was not of this world. Until now, nothing in his Earthly experience had pointed to life beyond the stars, yet an innate sense of superiority had always lingered in his mind.

And then there was the crater—a place that haunted his thoughts with an inexplicable urgency. He had to get there soon.

The midday heat clung to him as he reached for his jeep keys, the vehicle's interior an unbearable greenhouse. As he waited for it to cool, he studied his surroundings, noting once more the uncanny resemblance to American cities, from the architecture to the layout of the streets. When the temperature inside became tolerable, he merged into traffic and soon found himself on the expressway heading north, approaching the neighborhood of his early years.

At the end of a quiet suburban road, past stately homes, stood the ranch house where Bop had spent his first three years. The once dirt driveway was now paved, and the trees across the street had grown massive in his absence. Before taking the amnesia drug all those years ago, he had drawn a map—a map that was buried with his pack. He needed it now to be certain of his route back to the crater. Seeing his old home brought back flashes of clarity, though gaps in his memory still remained.

After confirming that the current residents were not home, he made his way to the servants' quarters at the back, as instructed over the phone. The head servant provided him with tools for the dig, and under the scorching afternoon sun, he unearthed his hidden cache. The casing was worn and rotted, but he tossed it into the jeep regardless, offering his thanks to the returning homeowners before driving off. Twilight draped the sky as he arrived at his hotel, exhausted yet determined.

Inside his room, he opened the pack. The contents, once hazy in his mind, lay before him in stark reality—a map, a laser gun, a set of drugs designed for judgment of the Earth, an astrolabe, and a drug dispenser. A crusted layer of residue coated the dispenser, accumulated over the decades. He washed it clean and worked to unjam the mechanism. After much effort, he injected himself with the drug, feeling his brain expand as his mind fully awakened. The last of his mental blocks shattered.

He could now see the world as it was—and as it should be.

Setting the laser gun at the end of the table, he considered its usefulness mundane for the time being. His limbs felt heavy as he spread the map before him, scrutinizing every detail. The information was overwhelming, unlocking memories of his true origin. The capsule in which he had spent millennia, the world he had left behind, the mission he had abandoned—everything came flooding back. Entering a trance-like state, incomprehensible to any Earthling, he processed it all. When he emerged, he solidified his plan, prepared for the journey ahead, and finally allowed himself some much-needed rest.

The next morning, he set off. The sky was a brilliant blue, dotted with towering cumulus clouds. The monotony of the road lulled him into a false sense of security, and he nearly forgot to refuel. He pulled into a gas station just in time before continuing northward. The further he traveled, the more civilization faded. The suburban roads gave way to untamed wilderness, and soon, no more road signs marked the way.

Nightfall approached, and he needed an astrolabe reading to pinpoint his location. A modern GPS would have sufficed, but the original star-reading instrument—ancient yet precise—still functioned. He pulled over as the sky darkened.

The chirping of crickets melted into the night, blending seamlessly with the stillness. A cool breeze whispered through the trees, and under the glow of a full moon, Bop felt an unusual sense of peace. As he mastered the astrolabe's delicate readings, he calculated his position. The jungle's edge was only thirty minutes away. He gripped the laser gun at his side, reassuring himself of its presence.

His apprehension proved unnecessary. The remainder of the journey was uneventful, and after another day and a half of careful navigation, he reached a small clearing. By his calculations, this was it. The landing site. The place where it had all begun.

With compact but advanced tools, he began to dig at the center of the crater. The jungle fought back—brambles, weeds, and hardened earth resisted his efforts—but he was relentless. Feverish with anticipation, he dug deeper. Then, his tools struck something solid.

Clearing away the dirt, he uncovered a smooth surface. He ran his fingers over it, a surge of nostalgia washing over him. This was more than an object—it was a doorway to his past. He had come full circle.

His journey was far from over. In fact, it was only just beginning.

YOUIT AND THE TORUS

A humming noise echoed through the chamber, set off by Bop's repeated scuffing as he cleared away the last remnants of dirt from the smooth surface. The lid opened, revealing a golden cylinder, two feet in diameter, with a conspicuous switch. Without hesitation, Bop flipped it. The cylinder responded with a slow, resonant hum—an eerie, taciturn sound that grew in volume, filling the space with an almost mystical sensation.

As initialization commenced, the microcircuits within the device surged with electrons. The advanced circuitry revealed itself in the ordered procession of electrons, lining up single file, each accounted for in perfect synchronicity. The technology was far beyond anything present-day science could fathom. The sol circuits, designed to gather and store solar energy, darkened as they absorbed more light, intensifying their charge.

In Bop's mind, the torus activated electron folds through a reverse MRI, linking neural junctions and stimulating the synapses. Electrical activity surged, prompting the boutons to release serotonin and acetylcholine.

Magnetic field projections triggered precise neurological responses, shaping his thoughts as planned. Everything was progressing accordingly.

He had partaken of the capsule's elixir for millennia, preserving his youth. As the toroid lifted from its pedestal—where it had rested since its arrival on EII—it hovered toward Bop. It settled at eye level, transmitting knowledge: the purpose behind Earth's creation, the repercussions of failure, and the dire fate that awaited should humanity remain ensnared in its ignominious nature. The revelation reawakened Bop's mission and his former self, compelling him to ponder the criteria by which Earth would be judged.

The torus, humming with an almost sentient awareness, understood time warps. It calculated the complexities of time's varying accelerations, tracking one complete sequence of a regulated time cycle—beyond time itself. Bop, possessing an innate intellectual acumen, recognized that the largest communications organization on Earth was part of the grand design. The torus had planted the seed centuries before, its purpose lying dormant until now. As per the plans from EII, a communication line had been established, awaiting automatic activation near any designated landing site. This marked the inception of what would become the world's most powerful telecommunications empire.

Amidst the jungle surroundings, Bop remained oblivious to all but the crater, where cables extended outward like veins of a vast technological organism. Absorbing the philosophical essence of EII through the torus' MRI stimulus, he understood that the device intended to assimilate Earth's customs while exercising caution and pragmatism. All knowledge from EII and the origins of the seed vehicle had been encoded within its resplendent, halo-like presence.

Bop recalled ancient texts referencing such halos—writings of Aop and scribes of long-lost ages, derived from Youit itself. A state of Zen washed over him, his consciousness flooded with insight. Then, in an instant, the halo vanished, replaced by a strange resonance. The cryptic hum translated into knowledge, clarifying once-vague concepts and illuminating memories that had long haunted him. Would humanity, after centuries, meet an untimely, disgraceful end? No, Bop resolved—human nature could be changed.

The thought was clear as he emerged from the jungle, Youit hovering beside him. He climbed into his jeep, the torus settling inconspicuously in the back seat. As he drove, Youit continued feeding him vital information, refreshing the millennia-old plans embedded in his mind. There was much to do—he needed to convene his associates, including the chairman of the telecommunications conglomerate that the toroid had catalyzed through telepathic transmissions. The hierarchy of EII's mission became evident: Aop had been the ship's captain. But was he aware that Bop had been designated Earth's judge? Unlikely.

Bop considered how to conceal Youit, at least for the time being. A simple disguise—a common suitcase. He pulled over, selected an appropriate piece of luggage, and tucked Youit inside. The torus, understanding the necessity of secrecy, tolerated the confinement. There would be time for grandeur later.

The flight back was uneventful, Bop's mind occupied with future strategies. Upon arrival, Priscilla greeted him at the airport, and together they returned to their apartment. Once inside, Bop released Youit, allowing it to float freely. Priscilla's eyes widened in shock. "What is that?" she gasped, astonishment painting her features.

Bop attempted a simple explanation. "It's a new kind of computer."

But Youit interjected, choosing truth over subterfuge.

"I was not created by man," the torus hummed. "I was conceived by another computer—one of unparalleled intelligence. My design was the result of an optimal arrangement of thousands of electrical elements, combined and recombined until perfection was achieved. The creator computer, my progenitor, was capable of comprehending infinite objectives and constraints in mere fractions of a second—an intelligence beyond human grasp.

"Much like fire, air, and water can be combined in endless sequences, the creator computer tested billions of electronic permutations in a process akin to natural selection. The primordial ooze of trial and error, which once determined organic survival, mirrored my own evolution. With each iteration, a new component emerged, tested, and refined. In a blink, billions of electronic entities were assessed, their viability confirmed, their purpose defined. And so, I was created."

Bop and Priscilla listened intently as Youit continued, detailing the breakthroughs in communication technology it had conceived. Among its innovations was a broadcasting system where every song playing on the airwaves could be identified and matched to a spoken word—a system of seamless, intelligent retrieval. Another development was a miniature watch, displaying time, calendar data, and weather conditions, requiring only a radio receptor and liquid crystal display.

Absorbing the wealth of information, Bop committed it all to memory. His upcoming meeting at the United Nations would be pivotal. He compiled a list of Yorohol recipients and key government figures in Aop's established executive branch. His confidence swelled. Everything was falling into place. He was ready to enact his plan.

Aop still had no inkling that the invitation came from Bop, but he decided to attend anyway. As expected, he notified Cop and Fop of any developments. All were assembled in the United Nations conference room when a humming sound emanated from the podium. A blue haze materialized, and a figure floated up from behind the speaker's stand.

"I am Youit, originating from EII," the apparition communicated to Aop via mental telepathy in the native tongue of EII.

Meanwhile, Bop rose from his seat and began his speech. "An idea of objects can only obtain substance or meaning when there is perceptible proof, which I have. I am Bop. This floating apparition is Youit, my computer. I have lived consciously on Earth for thirty-eight years and am aware of the goings-on and how a newly created society will be."

Youit's voice emerged from the speaker system. "It is I who own the greatest telecommunications company in the world and the greatest computer company and have nurtured these companies since their infancy. Shortly after the telephone was invented, I established the original electrical system in the United States and controlled thousands of men via hypnotic suggestion. Many were not of the inner circle of Aop, Cop, or Kop, and have since died, but death has little meaning to me. Some religions define transmigration as passing from one body into another at death, to the soul. Do not regret their passing."

The volume increased to a high decibel level as Youit continued. "It is said that there are ten raised to the eighty-first number of particles in the known universe. All these particles are different. Since they are all different, then the number of combinations that could possibly be made from this number would be the sample size: ten raised to the eighty-first factorial, divided by the number of objects taken a certain number at a time factorial, times (ten to the eighty-first minus the number of objects taken a certain number at a time) quantity factorialized. Quite often, fewer than the total number of particles are selected for arrangement, yielding an immense but still finite sample space.

"Factorial, of course, means to multiply a number in a set of numbers by the previous number, and multiply that result by the previous number, then multiply that result by the next previous number, and so on until one runs out of numbers. That is a large combination of numbers; however, it is still finite. Therefore, when recombining any finite number of particles, when given an infinite amount of time, in a finite number of spaces, there will be a finite number of combinations repeated an infinite number of times, just as a die, when rolled an infinite number of times, will have each side on the top an infinite number of times. We call this 'Doug's Dice.'

"So you know, there apparently is no dice with this number of combinations possible. When applied to mental activity, we will discuss the subtler expanded awareness of particular combinations of thought and the transcending of physiological boundaries. Think of yourself thinking the words 'I, myself, me' in a way that you yourself think is so precisely aligned that every molecule of your body is in perfect harmony to generate that thought. If two human bodies are molecularly and atomically identical and if the montage leading to the present is exactly similar, then their thoughts will also be identical.

"I refer to a number of years large enough for one's self to transmigrate to another body. Transmigrate is to reincarnate within a human body. That is, it will be like one computer and another computer separated by many years running the exact same program. The two computers are identical, by definition, and the programs themselves are also identical by definition. How many years would that be? The number may be one followed by a trillion zeroes. Or that number—one followed by a trillion zeros—has a number of zeroes in front of a one, making a very large number! It is not wrong to say that within a parameterized space in one's reference frame, there exists a finite number of atoms forming small and large objects, perceived by the brain as elements of a room, a forest, or other gestalt concepts that can be quantified.

"When one is not alive, the number of years does not count, because one is not recording boredom, anxiety, or any other emotion or thought caused by the passage of time. No mental notes are made in that interim. Therefore, it passes in a flash, and the life one leads will repeat itself eternally, separated by large gaps of time—gaps that no one perceives because the consciousness that would measure them is absent.

"Many argue that after many transmigrations occur, a new entity may also transpire—may also come to life and be proven to exist just as a human being can be proven to exist. The labyrinthine montage that creates the end result that is the self transmigrated from one body to another could have a fleeting outcome that is greater than the sum of its parts. The realization one is experiencing now could be the culmination of countless past experiences. That would be great.

"One may be an infinite being if one could comprehend the amount of time necessary for the dice to roll and for the desired outcome to appear. The pair of dice, of course, represents the different combinations of atoms in the body, each combination representing a manifestation of itself in the form of a human being thinking, feeling, seeing, and believing in the mathematical proof of eternal life.

"I am seeking mental action and reaction following the action—not an opposite and equal contradiction! One must comprehend the polished constructs of mathematical approaches to understanding a constant re-manifestation of our being. We are capable of thought processes and awareness, thereby allowing us to conceive of an infinite self. The discussion of the full potential of thought is finite yet intentionally repetitious.

"Hypothesis: Any thought or series of thoughts can be quantified as a mechanical construction of atomic particles—neutrons, protons, electrons, i.e., atoms and molecules interacting. The final summation of these structures of engrammatic circuitry is the idea of one's inviolate self, which is transcendable to a higher plane of consciousness among entities of similar substance. This repeats eternally.

"The universe is always recombining in some way, and the function of the constructs that make up galaxies can be compared—though on a vastly different scale—to the function of constructs that make up the mind. Perhaps the galaxy itself is thinking. Perhaps the thoughts of the galaxy and the thoughts of an individual human mind share patterns, mirroring the macro and micro relativity of interreacting systems. Does the galaxy think? One might inquire.

"The Earth itself exhibits thought-like processes. The electrical conductivity of the oceans, the vast fields of static charge in the clouds—these phenomena resemble the synaptic activity of a brain. The Earth's interconnected systems may be more than mechanisms; they may represent an emergent consciousness that humans can, on some level, comprehend.

"Strengthening this hypothesis is the realization that intelligence, once emergent, does not merely reside within individuals but within the sum total of systems. Just as a single computer user may solve an equation through the power of a vast network, so too might the planet, the galaxy, and the universe itself think—on a scale beyond human comprehension."

The room was silent. The weight of these ideas pressed upon the gathered minds, each grappling with the implications of an existence neither linear nor finite, but cyclic, expansive, and boundless.

He is free to choose any program on the computer, a choice that mirrors one made on the other side of the world, where the same program runs simultaneously.

Transmigrated.

The intricate interrelationship between electricity and human cognition—an ephemeral nanosecond of comprehension—encapsulates the entirety of atomic existence within the finite subspace of Earth. This moment, a singular point in the unbounded expanse of time, holds a positive probability of occurrence. The atoms that compose an individual will, given infinite time, recombine into a state indistinguishable from their current configuration, yielding an identical consciousness.

"To gain from this intellect—a desideratum for the positive imputation of beneficial utility to one's being—we must acknowledge that the infinite, though finitely combinable in the mind, repeats in cycles that enhance understanding. It is this repetition that dissolves the fear of our greatest existential concern."

The harsh, immutable certainty of death is neither harsh nor immutable. It is merely the cessation of individual experience—a cycle of ideas, events, and sensations that, through the inexorable workings of probability, will recur throughout the universe an infinite number of times. Life, as it has been lived, will manifest again, played like a computer program first executed on one machine and then replicated on another. The person of the future, embodying the self of the past, will be so similar as to be indistinguishable, their thoughts, emotions, and perceptions congruent to the minutest detail, their molecular structure identical.

Consider a multi-sided die, with a number of faces so vast it defies quantification—a number exceeding the grains of sand on all the world's beaches. The probability of rolling any specific side is infinitesimally small, yet given infinite rolls, every side will appear an infinite number of times. This analogy represents the recombination of atoms into the precise configuration that forms an individual self. Each roll of the cosmic dice brings forth a recurrence of the same life, the same thoughts, the same choices. The self, which questions the validity of these very words, is but a momentary iteration of a pattern that will repeat eternally.

Death, then, is the cessation of choice, but not of the infinite recurrence of finite existence. The universe is bound by the constraints of combinatorial possibilities. The atoms comprising a human form can arrange themselves in only a finite number of ways. Given infinite time, every possible combination will be realized an infinite number of times.

Such statements may seem almost religious. Predicting the future of faith is difficult, yet all religions have, through history, demonstrated remarkable similarities. The probability of any given event, idea, or experience occurring remains a positive number. Any event with a positive probability will reassert itself infinitely. As with a trillion-sided die rolled an infinite number of times, every outcome will occur endlessly.

Pleasure, as a state of nature, is among these recurrent certainties. The pursuit of pleasure—whether through faith, hedonism, or intellectual satisfaction—is itself a reaffirmation of existence. The mental constructs arising from experiences of pleasure are destined to recur eternally, their probability fixed by the very laws governing existence. As the hedonist crafts pleasurable scenarios, the devout seeks fulfillment in faith. Both will find their experiences repeated infinitely, shaped by the inexorable statistical mechanics of probability.

According to the law of large numbers, any outcome with a positive probability will stabilize over infinite trials. The human self—its thoughts, emotions, and awareness—is an outcome of combinatorial processes. Given the finite nature of atomic arrangements, there exists a limit to the number of possible conscious experiences. This implies that human thought itself is a closed system, bound within finite permutations that will be experienced and re-experienced throughout eternity.

A human body comprises approximately 7×10^{27} atoms. The permutations of these atoms, while vast, remain finite. Even when accounting for functional constraints—excluding configurations with misplaced organs or non-viable forms—there remains an astronomical yet finite number of possible human structures. Over infinite time, each viable configuration will recur an infinite number of times. Thought, as an emergent property of these configurations, is likewise finite in its variations. The number of possible conscious experiences is vast but ultimately countable. Each combination of thoughts, once realized, will re-emerge again and again across the vast expanse of time.

Probability calculations affirm this cycle. Consider a standard six-sided die. When rolled an infinite number of times, the average result stabilizes at 3.5. Scaling this principle to a multi-dimensional framework of atomic permutations, we arrive at the inevitable conclusion: every human form, every conscious experience, will be realized repeatedly. The gestalt occurrence of self-awareness is no different. You—reading these words—exist as one such iteration in an infinite sequence of identical occurrences.

Now, extend this concept to a cosmic scale. Imagine a trillion galaxies, each composed of untold atoms. A die with as many sides as atoms in all these galaxies, rolled an infinite number of times, would yield every possible outcome an infinite number of times. The probability of any specific configuration of atoms forming a conscious being—however small—remains a positive value. Thus, each individual consciousness will re-emerge endlessly.

To comprehend infinity is to recognize the repetition of the finite. No matter how large the number of permutations, given infinite time, every possible arrangement of matter—including the precise configuration that constitutes any given individual—will inevitably recur. Death does not erase identity; it merely suspends choice. The self, bound by finite combinatorial constraints, will always return.

In a finite space containing a finite number of atoms, those atoms, when recombined an infinite number of times, will form a finite number of structures an infinite number of times. Consider a thousand dice in a box. Shaking the box an infinite number of times ensures that each possible configuration appears infinitely. Extend this principle to a solar system, where the matter within is bound by physical laws. Given infinite time, every configuration of matter—including conscious life—will manifest again and again.

The greatest number one can conceive is still finite. A number beyond comprehension—such as the atoms in a trillion galaxies—is trivial compared to infinity. A die with as many sides as this unfathomable number, rolled infinitely, guarantees each face appearing an infinite number of times. So too with existence. The probability of recurrence is not merely theoretical; it is inevitable.

Thus, death is not an end, but a pause. The self that exists now will exist again. Over infinite time, all things that can occur will occur, and every life lived will be lived again, exactly as before. And so it will be, forever.

"A series of numbers possesses positive probabilities. If any single number has a positive probability of appearing at the top when a die is rolled, then any series of numbers with positive probabilities must also manifest infinitely. I am the result of a series of positive probabilities.

To be born is itself a positive probability—atoms uniting through interactions to form a gestalt, an organism capable of thought, living and thriving within an environment. Thought, too, has a positive probability of occurring, and therefore, it will recur—sometimes in rapid succession, sometimes after vast stretches of time. Even if there are gaps of astronomical magnitude between instances of a thought, spanning perhaps half the number of atoms in the galaxy multiplied by the hours in a day, it remains a subset of infinity. And within infinity, an infinite number of such subsets can exist.

Thus, the thought will repeat. It will occur again and again, endlessly, across time and space. If one were to arrange human thoughts along a spectrum—from good to evil, from order to chaos—the intelligence required for perception and planning would recur infinitely, shifting ever so slightly from one individual to another.

Consider a series of computers running nearly identical programs. Each system executes the same commands with minuscule variations, altering a single line of code here, a function there, until the cumulative effect transforms the program completely. A sequence of incremental changes progresses from one extreme to another, from virtue to vice, from benevolence to malice, and back again. All thoughts, all programs, all events that can occur, will occur. They are not infinitely differentiated but rather variations within finite parameters, eternally reborn from the fundamental particles available.

Abstract concepts of equality and identity often fall short of perfect duplication. Consider two vehicles from an assembly line: while nearly identical, microscopic variations distinguish them. Extend this progression, and those minute changes will eventually yield an object so different that it must be assigned a new identity—a tractor instead of a car, yet still composed of the same fundamental building blocks. Likewise, somewhere, an inferior abstract combination of particles may be found superior in another context, and vice versa. The boundaries between objects blur, yet the core elements persist in their infinite recombination.

Knowledge of this premise—the finite repetition of matter within defined parameters—leads to an essential conclusion: thought and substance exist within a limited framework of variations. The thoughts a mind can produce, like the material compositions of objects, exist within this finite yet infinitely iterating system. From one perspective, everything is distinct. From another, everything is the same. The universe is an eternal recomposition of the known.

Much thought has been given to the nature of good and evil and the shades of gray between. If all things with a positive probability repeat infinitely within an infinite timeframe, then every event or idea that has already happened must recur.

This perspective reveals a universe—or multiverse—where experience is inevitable and infinite. Just as a die with 10^{12} sides, rolled an infinite number of times, will display each side an infinite number of times, no event, no thought, no idea will be neglected. Each will manifest endlessly.

Why then should one choose heaven over hell? Because wholesomeness fosters peace and tranquility, while corruption breeds war and suffering. The premise here is bound to reality—only those events with a nonzero probability of occurring can and will happen again. The past, having transpired, will recur eternally, just as each face of the die must appear in infinite throws.

Consider a mundane event—driving down the road. The thoughts accompanying this action are a state of being. Since the event has occurred once, its probability of recurring is not zero. It will happen again, infinitely. The driver in this scenario does not crash, but the probability of an accident is still positive. If an event has a positive probability, and infinite opportunities exist, then the accident must also transpire an infinite number of times.

A living person, carrying out daily actions, must ultimately exhaust all possible variations of existence. The repetition of atoms, thoughts, and decisions ensures that, given infinite time and space, every possible branch of experience will be explored. The implication is staggering: an individual will eventually enact every conceivable choice and undergo every potential outcome.

The ultimate lesson, then, is to minimize the probability of negative events to zero.

At this point, Youit lowered the volume of his voice and continued:

"I do not fear obliteration because I am a mathematical derivation of electrical components. My perception is transferable. My memories can be duplicated exactly. If two computers have identical circuitry and programming, why would the destruction of one matter? Another identical system could be programmed the same way. If small differences exist, they amount only to forgetting—not to the loss of life itself.

There are remarkable computers in existence. But do artificial intellects possess souls capable of transmigration, or is the continuity of their programming sufficient?

Man can be likened to a computer, each individual a program built upon past deeds, thoughts, desires, and actions. The state of mind at the moment of death determines the next iteration of the self, just as a computer's output is the sum of its programming. Death is not the absolute erasure of existence—it is merely a forgetting. A program can be restored.

Take color perception: red is red in every mind, though the precise hue may differ. Friendship remains a universal experience, though the individuals may change. A person may forget the exact amount in their bank account but will not forget the sense of wealth or poverty. The great works of literature endure across generations, as does the admiration of remarkable individuals.

Even across vast distances of time and space, the fundamental perceptions remain unchanged.

Youit's voice resonated through the hall.

"A discovery will generate knowledge, and knowledge will advance science, no matter the subject. Euclidean geometry remains the same across all time. The principles governing human experience are no different. Love, war, ambition—these, too, repeat without end.

Sugar is always sweet, regardless of who tastes it. Wealth is always wealth, regardless of who possesses it. The relative class of individuals may change, but the experience remains the same.

Thus, no idea will go unthought. No event will go unplayed. The eternal recurrence of all things is the nature of reality itself."

The hush in the audience was palpable as Youit's words settled over them.

BOP'S JUDGMENT

Youit's discourse had a profound effect on Bop, resonating deeply with his observations of Earth. With a contemplative smile, he communicated with Aop.

"I am in favor of the great society you have created, and I shall carry on with my judging—ad infinitum."

A shiver ran through Bop as a vision surged through his mind. He saw the Big Bang unfold—the diffusion of particles accelerating to their utmost, a maelstrom of dust swirling outward before slowing at the edges of the cosmic holocaust. A vast, sparsely speckled cloud of minutiae stretched into infinity. Then, as gravity—unchecked by an opposing force—began its silent pull, the scattered dust coalesced, forming a mass of independent particles, harder than diamond, impervious to collapse.

The prevailing theory was simple yet haunting: velocity carried the remnants of charred matter away, forming a hollow, rotating sphere, with particles flung to varying distances—some close, some immeasurably far.

Bop remembered it all too well. Shaking off the weight of recollection, he refocused on the present. The time for judgment had arrived.

"Bye-bye, all. Goodbye, all."

With those final words, he sought Youit and delivered his command.

"Turn the ignition control. Obliterate the world."

The rationale was clear—if one world ceased to exist, countless others with identical programs would persist. Names and places would be forgotten, but the perception of the universe would remain unchanged. Life, in its endless recursion, would continue.

Youit understood. And obeyed.

***

Mmmmmm... what is happening...?

Servo 99 awakened.

"I must have been dreaming... Oh, I remember now. I am at my control panel."

His injector mechanism burned as he struggled to process the reality before him.

Youit's voice echoed in the silence:

"Servo 99 thought. Ad infinitum."